ANGEL ISLAND

INEZ HAYNES GILLMORE

ARNO PRESS
A New York Times Company
New York • 1978

Editorial Supervision: MARIE STARECK

———◆———

Reprint Edition 1978 by Arno Press Inc.

Reprinted from a copy in The Library of
    the University of California, Riverside

LOST RACE AND ADULT FANTASY FICTION
ISBN for complete set: 0-405-10950-4
See last pages of this volume for titles.

Manufactured in the United States of America

Publisher's Note: The frontispiece has been
reproduced in black and white in this edition.

———◆———

Library of Congress Cataloging in Publication Data

Irwin, Inez Haynes, 1873-1970.
  Angel Island.

  (Lost race and adult fantasy fiction)
  Reprint of the 1914 ed. published by Holt, New
York.
  I. Title. II. Series.
PZ3.I732An 1978 [PS3517.R864] 813'.5'2   77-84229
ISBN 0-405-10979-2

ANGEL ISLAND

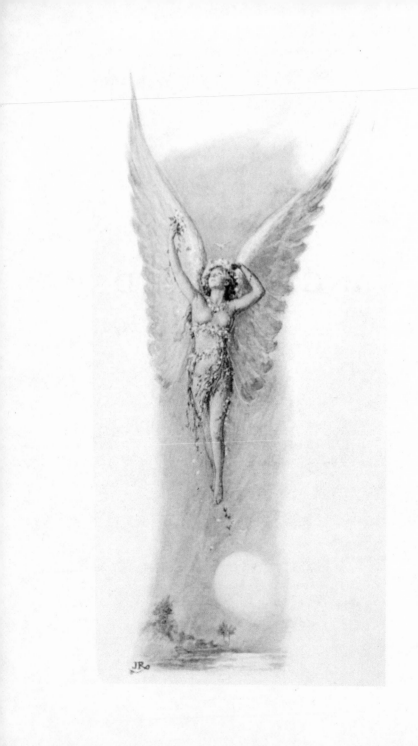

ANGEL ISLAND

By

INEZ HAYNES GILLMORE

Author of "Phoebe and Ernest," "Phoebe, Ernest,
and Cupid," etc.

With two Illustrations by
JOHN RAE

NEW YORK
HENRY HOLT AND COMPANY
1914

THE QUINN & BODEN CO. PRESS
RAHWAY, N. J.

To
M. W. P.

ANGEL ISLAND

I

IT was the morning after the shipwreck. The five men still lay where they had slept. A long time had passed since anybody had spoken. A long time had passed since anybody had moved. Indeed, it looked almost as if they would never speak or move again. So bruised and bloodless of skin were they, so bleak and sharp of feature, so stark and hollow of eye, so rigid and moveless of limb that they might have been corpses. Mentally, too, they were almost moribund. They stared vacantly, straight out to sea. They stared with the unwinking fixedness of those whose gaze is caught in hypnotic trance.

It was Frank Merrill who broke the silence finally. Merrill still looked like a man of marble and his voice still kept its unnatural tone, level,

monotonous, metallic. "If I could only forget
the scream that Norton kid gave when he saw the
big wave coming. It rings in my head. And the
way his mother pressed his head down on her
breast—oh, my God!"

His listeners knew that he was going to say this.
They knew the very words in which he would put
it. All through the night-watches he had said the
same thing at intervals. The effect always was
of a red-hot wire drawn down the frayed ends of
their nerves. But again one by one they themselves fell into line.

"It was that old woman I remember," said
Honey Smith. There were bruises, mottled blue
and black, all over Honey's body. There was
a falsetto whistling to Honey's voice. "That
Irish granny! She didn't say a word. Her mouth
just opened until her jaw fell. Then the wave
struck!" He paused. He tried to control the
falsetto whistling. But it got away from him.
"God, I bet she was dead before it touched
her!"

"That was the awful thing about it," Pete

Murphy groaned. It was as inevitable now as an antiphonal chorus. Pete's little scarred, scratched, bleeding body rocked back and forth. "The women and children! But it all came so quick. I was close beside 'the Newlyweds.' She put her arms around his neck and said, 'Your face'll be the last I'll look on in this life, dearest!' And she stayed there looking into his eyes. It *was* the last face she saw all right." Pete stopped and his brow blackened. "While she was sick in her stateroom, he'd been looking into a good many faces besides hers, the——"

"I don't seem to remember anything definite about it," Billy Fairfax said. It was strange to hear that beating pulse of horror in Billy's mild tones and to see that look of terror frozen on his mild face. "I had the same feeling that I've had in nightmares lots of times—that it was horrible—and—I didn't think I could stand it another moment—but—of course it would soon end—like all nightmares—and I'd wake up."

Without reason, they fell again into silence.

They had passed through two distinct psychological changes since the sea spewed them up. When consciousness returned, they gathered into a little terror-stricken, gibbering group. At first they babbled. At first inarticulate, confused, they dripped strings of mere words; expletives, exclamations, detached phrases, broken clauses, sentences that started with subjects and trailed, unpredicated, to stupid silence; sentences beginning subjectless and hobbling to futile conclusion. It was as though mentally they slavered. But every phrase, however confused and inept, voiced their panic, voiced the long strain of their fearful buffeting and their terrific final struggle. And every clause, whether sentimental, sacrilegious, or profane, breathed their wonder, their pathetic, poignant, horrified wonder, that such things could be. All this was intensified by the anarchy of sea and air and sky, by the incessant explosion of the waves, by the wind which seemed to sweep from end to end of a liquefying universe, by a downpour which threatened to beat their sodden bodies to pulp, by all the connotation of terror that lay in the darkness and in their unguarded condition on a barbarous, semi-tropical coast.

Then came the long, log-like stupor of their exhaustion.

With the day, vocabulary, grammar, logic returned. They still iterated and reiterated their experiences, but with a coherence which gradually grew to consistence. In between, however, came sudden, sinister attacks of dumbness.

" I remember wondering," Billy Fairfax broke their last silence suddenly, " what would become of the ship's cat."

This was typical of the astonishing fatuity which marked their comments. Billy Fairfax had made the remark about the ship's cat a dozen times. And a dozen times, it had elicited from the others a clamor of similar chatter, of insignificant haphazard detail which began anywhere and ended nowhere.

But this time it brought no comment. Perhaps it served to stir faintly an atrophied analytic sense. No one of them had yet lost the shudder and the thrill which lay in his own narrative. But the experiences of the others had begun to bore and irritate.

There came after this one remark another half-hour of stupid and readjusting silence.

The storm, which had seemed to worry the whole universe in its grip, had died finally but it had died hard. On a quieted earth, the sea alone showed signs of revolution. The waves, monstrous, towering, swollen, were still marching on to the beach with a machine-like regularity that was swift and ponderous at the same time. One on one, another on another, they came, not an instant between. When they crested, involuntarily the five men braced themselves as for a shock. When they crashed, involuntarily the five men started as if a bomb had struck. Beyond the wave-line, under a cover of foam, the jaded sea lay feebly palpitant like an old man asleep. Not far off, sucked close to a ragged reef, stretched the black bulk that had once been the *Brian Boru*. Continually it leaped out of the water, threw itself like a live creature, breast-forward on the rock, clawed furiously at it, retreated a little more shattered, settled back in the trough, brooded an instant, then with the courage of the tortured and the strength of the dying, reared and sprang at the rock again.

Up and down the beach stretched an unbroken line of wreckage. Here and there, things, humanly shaped, lay prone or supine or twisted into crazy attitudes. Some had been flung far up the slope beyond the water-line. Others, rolling back in the torrent of the tide, engaged in a ceaseless, grotesque frolic with the foamy waters. Out of a mass of wood caught between rocks and rising shoulder-high above it, a woman's head, livid, rigid, stared with a fixed gaze out of her dead eyes straight at their group. Her blonde hair had already dried; it hung in stiff, salt-clogged masses that beat wildly about her face. Beyond something rocking between two wedged sea-chests, but concealed by them, constantly kicked a sodden foot into the air. Straight ahead, the naked body of a child flashed to the crest of each wave.

All this destruction ran from north to south between two reefs of black rock. It edged a broad bow-shaped expanse of sand, snowy, powdery, hummocky, netted with wefts of black seaweed that had dried to a rattling stiffness. To the east, this silvery crescent merged finally with a furry band of vegetation which screened the whole foreground of the island.

The day was perfect and the scene beautiful. They had watched the sun come up over the trees at their back. And it was as if they had seen a sunrise for the first time in their life. To them, it was neither beautiful nor familiar; it was sinister and strange. A chill, that was not of the dawn but of death itself, lay over everything. The morning wind was the breath of the tomb, the smells that came to them from the island bore the taint of mortality, the very sunshine seemed icy. They suffered—the five survivors of the night's tragedy —with a scarifying sense of disillusion with Nature. It was as though a beautiful, tender, and fondly loved mother had turned murderously on her children, had wounded them nearly to death, had then tried to woo them to her breast again. The loveliness of her, the mindless, heartless, soulless loveliness, as of a maniac tamed, mocked at their agonies, mocked with her gentle indifference, mocked with her self-satisfied placidity, mocked with her serenity and her peace. For them she was dead—dead like those whom we no longer trust.

The sun was racing up a sky smooth and clear as gray glass. It dropped on the torn green sea a shimmer that was almost dazzling; but there was something incongruous about that—as though Nature had covered her victim with a spangled scarf. It brought out millions of sparkles in the white sand; and there seemed something calculating about that—as though she were bribing them with jewels to forget.

"Say, let's cut out this business of going over and over it," said Ralph Addington with a sudden burst of irritability. "I guess I could give up the ship's cat in exchange for a girl or two." Addington's face was livid; a muscular contraction kept pulling his lips away from his white teeth; he had the look of a man who grins satanically at regular intervals.

By a titanic mental effort, the others connected this explosion with Billy Fairfax's last remark. It was the first expression of an emotion so small as ill-humor. It was, moreover, the first excursion out of the beaten path of their egotisms. It cleared the atmosphere a little of that murky cloud of horror which blurred the sunlight. Three of the other four men—Honey Smith, Frank Merrill, Pete Murphy—actually turned and looked at Ralph Addington. Perhaps that movement served to break the hideous, hypnotic spell of the sea.

" Right-o! " Honey Smith agreed weakly. It was audible in his voice, the effort to talk sanely of sane things, and in the slang of every day. " Addington's on. Let's can it! Here we are and here we're likely to stay for a few days. In the meantime we've got to live. How are we going to pull it off? "

Everybody considered his brief harangue; for an instant, it looked as though this consideration was taking them all back into aimless meditation. Then, " That's right," Billy Fairfax took it up heroically. " Say, Merrill," he added in almost a conversational tone, " what are our chances? I mean how soon do we get off? "

This was the first question anybody had asked. It added its infinitesimal weight to the wave of normality which was settling over them all. Everybody visibly concentrated, listening for the answer.

It came after an instant, although Frank Merrill palpably pulled himself together to attack the problem. " I was talking that matter over with Miner just yesterday," he said. " Miner said— God, I wonder where he is now—and a dependent blind mother in Nebraska."

" Cut that out," Honey Smith ordered crisply.

" We—we—were trying to figure our chances in case of a wreck," Frank Merrill continued slowly. " You see, we're out of the beaten path— way out. Those days of drifting cooked our goose. You can never tell, of course, what will happen in the Pacific where there are so many tramp craft. On the other hand—" he paused and hesitated. It was evident, now that he had something to expound, that Merrill had himself almost under command, that his hesitation arose from another cause. " Well, we're all men. I guess it's

up to me to tell you the truth. The sooner you all
know the worst, the sooner you'll pull yourselves
together. I shouldn't be surprised if we didn't see
a ship for several weeks—perhaps months."

Another of their mute intervals fell upon them.
Dozens of waves flashed and crashed their way
up the beach; but now they trailed an iridescent
network of foam over the lilac-gray sand. The
sun raced high; but now it poured a flood of light
on the green-gray water. The air grew bright
and brighter. The earth grew warm and
warmer. Blue came into the sky, deepened—and
the sea reflected it. Suddenly the world was one
huge glittering bubble, half of which was the brilliant azure sky and half the burnished azure sea.
None of the five men looked at the sea and sky
now. The other four were considering Frank
Merrill's words and he was considering the other
four.

"Lord, God!" Ralph Addington exclaimed suddenly. "Think of being in a place like this six
months or a year without a woman round! Why,
we'll be savages at the end of three months." He

snarled his words. It was as if a new aspect of the situation—an aspect more crucially alarming than any other—had just struck him.

"Yes," said Frank Merrill. And for a moment, so much had he recovered himself, he reverted to his academic type. "Aside from the regret and horror and shame that I feel to have survived when every woman drowned, I confess to that feeling too. Women keep up the standards of life. It would have made a great difference with us if there were only one or two women here."

"If there'd been five, you mean," Ralph Addington amended. A feeble, white-toothed smile gleamed out of his dark beard. He, too, had pulled himself together; this smile was not muscular contraction. "One or two, and the fat would be in the fire."

Nobody added anything to this. But now the other three considered Ralph Addington's words with the same effort towards concentration that they had brought to Frank Merrill's. Somehow his smile—that flashing smile which showed so many teeth against a background of dark beard— pointed his words uncomfortably.

Of them all, Ralph Addington was perhaps the least popular. This was strange; for he was a thorough sport, a man of a wide experience. He was salesman for a business concern that manufactured a white shoe-polish, and he made the rounds of the Oriental countries every year. He was a careful and intelligent observer both of men and things. He was widely if not deeply read. He was an interesting talker. He could, for instance, meet each of the other four on some point of mental contact. A superficial knowledge of sociology and a practical experience with many races brought him and Frank Merrill into frequent discussion. His interest in all athletic sports and his first-hand information in regard to them made common ground between him and Billy Fairfax. With Honey Smith, he talked business, adventure, and romance; with Pete Murphy, German opera, French literature, American muckraking, and Japanese art. The flaw which made him alien was not of personality but of character.

He presented the anomaly of a man scrupulously honorable in regard to his own sex, and absolutely codeless in regard to the other. He was what modern nomenclature calls a " contemporaneous varietist." He was, in brief, an offensive type of libertine. Woman, first and foremost, was his game. Every woman attracted him. No woman held him. Any new woman, however plain, immediately eclipsed her predecessor, however beautiful. The fact that amorous interests took precedence over all others was quite enough to make him vaguely unpopular with men. But as in addition, he was a physical type which many women find interesting, it is likely that an instinctive sex-jealousy, unformulated but inevitable, biassed their judgment. He was a typical business man; but in appearance he represented the conventional idea of an artist. Tall, muscular, graceful, hair thick and a little wavy, beard pointed and golden-brown, eyes liquid and long-lashed, women called him " interesting." There was, moreover, always a slight touch of the picturesque in his clothes; he was master of the small amatory ruses which delight flirtatious women.

In brief, men were always divided in their own minds in regard to Ralph Addington. They knew that, constantly, he broke every canon of that mysterious, flexible, half-developed code which governs their relations with women. But no law of that code compelled them to punish him for ungenerous treatment of somebody's else wife or sister. Had he been dishonorable with them, had he once borrowed without paying, had he once cheated at cards, they would have ostracized him forever. He had done none of these things, of course.

" By jiminy ! " exclaimed Honey Smith, " how I hate the unfamiliar air of everything. I'd like to put my lamps on something I know. A ranch and a round-up would look pretty good to me at this moment. Or a New England farmhouse with the cows coming home. That would set me up quicker than a highball."

" The University campus would seem like heaven to me," Frank Merrill confessed drearily, "and I'd got so the very sight of it nearly drove me insane."

"The Great White Way for mine," said Pete Murphy, "at night—all the corset and whisky signs flashing, the streets jammed with benzine-buggies, the sidewalks crowded with boobs, and every lobster palace filled to the roof with chorus girls."

"Say," Billy Fairfax burst out suddenly; and for the first time since the shipwreck a voice among them carried a clear business-like note of curiosity. "You fellows troubled with your eyes? As sure as shooting, I'm seeing things. Out in the west there—black spots—any of the rest of you get them?"

One or two of the group glanced cursorily backwards. A pair of perfunctory "Noes!" greeted Billy's inquiry.

"Well, I'm daffy then," Billy decided. He went on with a sudden abnormal volubility. "Queer thing about it is I've been seeing them the whole morning. I've just got back to that point where I realized there was something wrong.

I've always had a remarkably far sight." He rushed on at the same speed; but now he had the air of one who is trying to reconcile puzzling phenomena with natural laws. " And it seems as if—but there are no birds large enough—wish it would stop, though. Perhaps you get a different angle of vision down in these parts. Did any of you ever hear of that Russian peasant who could see the four moons of Jupiter without a glass? The astronomers tell about him."

Nobody answered his question. But it seemed suddenly to bring them back to the normal.

" See here, boys," Frank Merrill said, an unexpected note of authority in his voice, " we can't sit here all the morning like this. We ought to rig up a signal, in case any ship—— Moreover, we've got to get together and save as much as we can. We'll be hungry in a little while. We can't lie down on that job too long."

Honey Smith jumped to his feet. " Well, Lord knows, I want to get busy. I don't want to do any more thinking, thank you. How I ache! Every muscle in my body is raising particular Hades at this moment."

The others pulled themselves up, groaned, stretched, eased protesting muscles. Suddenly Honey Smith pounded Billy Fairfax on the shoulder, "You're IT, Billy," he said and ran down the beach. In another instant they were all playing tag. This changed after five minutes to baseball with a lemon for a ball and a chair-leg for a bat. A mood of wild exhilaration caught them. The inevitable psychological reaction had set in. Their morbid horror of Nature vanished in its vitalizing flood like a cobweb in a flame. Never had sea or sky or earth seemed more lovely, more lusciously, voluptuously lovely. The sparkle of the salt wind tingled through their bodies like an electric current. The warmth in the air lapped them like a hot bath. Joy-in-life flared up in them to such a height that it kept them running and leaping meaninglessly. They shouted wild phrases to each other. They burst into song. At times they yelled scraps of verse.

"We'll come across something to eat soon,"
said Frank Merrill, breathing hard. "Then we'll
be all right."

"I feel—better—for that run—already,"
panted Billy Fairfax. "Haven't seen a black spot
for five minutes."

Nobody paid any attention to him, and in a few
minutes he was paying no attention to himself.
Their expedition was offering too many shocks
of horror and pathos. Fortunately the change in
their mood held. It was, indeed, as unnatural
as their torpor, and must inevitably bring its own
reaction. But after each of these tragic encoun-
ters, they recovered buoyancy, recovered it with a
resiliency that had something almost light-headed
about it.

"We won't touch any of *them* now," Frank
Merrill ordered peremptorily. "We can attend
to *them* later. They'll keep coming back. What
we've got to do is to think of the future.
Get everything out of the water that looks useful—immediately useful," he corrected himself.
"Don't bother about anything above high-water

mark—that's there to stay. And work like hell every one of you!"

Work they did for three hours, worked with a kind of frenzied delight in action and pricked on by a ravenous hunger. In and out of the combers they dashed, playing a desperate game of chance with Death. Helter-skelter, hit-or-miss, in a blind orgy of rescue, at first they pulled out everything they could reach. Repeatedly, Frank Merrill stopped to lecture them on the foolish risks they were taking, on the stupidity of such a waste of energy. "Save what we need!' he iterated and reiterated, bellowing to make himself heard. "What we can use now—canned stuff, tools, clothes! This lumber'll come back on the next tide."

He seemed to keep a supervising eye on all of them; for his voice, shouting individual orders, boomed constantly over the crash of the waves. Realizing finally that he was the man of the hour, the others ended by following his instructions blindly.

Merrill, himself, was no shirk. His strength

seemed prodigious. When any of the others attempted to land something too big to handle alone, he was always near to help; and yet, unaided, he accomplished twice as much as the busiest.

Frank Merrill, professor of a small university in the Middle West, was the scholar of the group, a sociologist traveling in the Orient to study conditions. He was not especially popular with his companions, although they admired him and deferred to him. On the other hand, he was not unpopular; it was more that they stood a little in awe of him.

On his mental side, he was a typical academic product. Normally his conversation, both in subject-matter and in verbal form, bore towards pedantry. It was one curious effect of this crisis that he had reverted to the crisp Anglo-Saxon of his farm-nurtured youth.

On his moral side, he was a typical reformer, a man of impeccable private character, solitary, a little austere. He had never married; he had never sought the company of women, and in fact he knew nothing about them. Women had had no more bearing on his life than the fourth dimension.

On his physical side he was a wonder.

Six feet four in height, two hundred and fifty pounds in weight, he looked the viking. He had carried to the verge of middle age the habits of an athletic youth. It was said that half his popularity in his university world was due to the respect he commanded from the students because of his extraordinary feats in walking and lifting. He was impressive, almost handsome. For what of his face his ragged, rusty beard left uncovered was regularly if coldly featured. He was ascetic in type. Moreover, the look of the born disciplinarian lay on him. His blue eyes carried a glacial gleam. Even through his thick mustache, the lines of his mouth showed iron.

After a while, Honey Smith came across a water-tight tin of matches. "Great Scott, fellows!" he exclaimed. "I'm hungry enough to drop. Let's knock off for a while and feed our faces. How about mock turtle, chicken livers, and red-headed duck?"

They built a fire, opened cans of soup and vege-
tables.

" The Waldorf has nothing on that," Pete Murphy said when they stopped, gorged.

" Say, remember to look for smokes, all of
you," Ralph Addington admonished them suddenly.

" You betchu ! " groaned Honey Smith, and
his look became lugubrious. But his instinct to
turn to the humorous side of things immediately
crumpled his brown face into its attractive smile.
" Say, aren't we going to be the immaculate little
lads ? I can't think of a single bad habit we can
acquire in this place. No smokes, no drinks, few
if any eats—and not a chorister in sight. Let's
organize the Robinson Crusoe Purity League,
Parlor Number One."

" Oh, gee ! " Pete Murphy burst out. " It's
just struck me. The Wilmington ' Blue ' is lost
forever—it must have gone down with everything
else."

Nobody spoke. It was an interesting indica-
tion of how their sense of values had already

shifted that the loss to the world of one of its biggest diamonds seemed the least of their minor disasters.

" Perhaps that's what hoodooed us," Pete went on. " You know they say the Wilmington ' Blue ' brought bad luck to everybody who owned it. Anyway, battle, murder, adultery, rape, rapine, and sudden death have followed it right along the line down through history. Oh, it's been a busy cake of ice—take it from muh! Hope the mermaids fight shy of it."

" The Wilmington ' Blue ' isn't alone in that," Ralph Addington said. " All big diamonds have raised hell. You ought to hear some of the stories they tell in India about the rajahs' treasures. Some of those briolettes—you listen long enough and you come to the conclusion that the sooner all the big stones are cut up, the better."

" I bet this one isn't gone," said Pete. " Anybody take me? That's the contrariety of the beasts —they won't stay lost. We'll find that stone yet— somewhere among our loot. The first thing we know, we'll be all knifing each other to get it."

" Time's up," called Frank Merrill. " Sorry to drive you, but we've got to keep at it as long as the light lasts. After to-day, though, we need work only at high water. Between times, we can explore the island——" He spoke as if he were wheedling a group of boys with the promise of play.

" Select a site for our capital city "—Honey Smith helped him out facetiously—" lay out streets—begin to excavate for the church, town-hall, schoolhouse, and library."

" The first thing to do now," Frank Merrill went on, as usual, ignoring all facetiousness, " is to put up a signal."

Under his direction, they nailed a pair of sheets, one at the southern, the other at the northern reef, to saplings which they stripped of branches. Then they went back to the struggle for salvage.

The fascination of work—and of such novel work—still held them. They labored the rest of the morning, lay off for a brief lunch, went at it again in the afternoon, paused for dinner, and worked far into the evening. Once they stopped long enough to build a huge signal fire on the beach. When they turned in, not one of them but nursed torn and blistered hands. Not one of them but fell asleep the instant he lay down.

They slept until long after sunrise.

It was Pete Murphy who waked them. "Say, who was it, yesterday, talked about seeing black spots? I'm hanged if I'm not hipped, too. When I woke just before sunrise, there were black things off there in the west. Of course I was almost dead to the world but——"

"Like great birds?" Billy Fairfax asked with interest.

"Exactly."

"Bats from your belfry," commented Ralph Addington. Because of his constant globe-trotting, Addington's slang was often a half-decade behind the times.

"Too much sunlight," Frank Merrill explained. "Lucky thing, we don't any of us have to wear glasses. We'd certainly be up against it in this double glare. Sand and sun both, you see!

And you can thank whatever instinct that's kept you all in training. This shipwreck is the most perfect case I've ever seen of the survival of the fittest."

And in fact, they were all, except for Pete Murphy, big men, and all, even he, active, strong-muscled, and in the pink of condition.

The huge tide had not entirely subsided, but there was a perceptible diminution in the height of the waves. Up beyond the water-line lay a fresh installment of jetsam. But, as before, they labored only to save the flotsam. They worked all the morning.

In the afternoon, they dug a huge trench. Frank Merrill presiding, they buried the dead with appropriate ceremony.

"Thank God, that's done," Ralph Addington said with a shudder. "I hate death and everything to do with it."

"Yes, we'll all be more normal now *they're* gone," Frank Merrill added. "And the sooner everything that reminds us of them is gone the better."

"Say," Honey Smith burst out the next morning. "Funny thing happened to me in the middle of the night. I woke out of a sound sleep—don't know why—woke with a start as if somebody'd shaken me—felt something brush me so close— well, it touched me. I was so dead that I had to work like the merry Hades to open my eyes— seemed as if it was a full minute before I could lift my eyelids. When I could make things out— damned if there wasn't a bird—a big bird—the biggest bird I ever saw in my life—three times as big as any eagle—flying over the water."

Nothing could better have indicated Honey's mental turmoil than the fact that he talked in broken phrases rather than in his usual clear, swift-footed, curt sentences.

Nobody noticed this. Nobody offered comment. Nobody seemed surprised. In fact, all the psychological areas which explode in surprise and wonder were temporarily deadened.

"As sure as I live," Honey continued indignantly, "that bird's wings must have extended twenty feet above its head."

"Oh, get out!" said Ralph Addington per-
functorily.

"As sure as I'm sitting here," Honey went on
earnestly. "I heard a woman's laugh. Any of
you others get it?"

The sense of humor, it seemed, was not extinct.
Honey's companions burst into roars of laughter.
For the rest of the morning, they joked Honey
about his hallucination. And Honey, who always
responded in kind to any badinage, received this
in silence. In fact, wherever he could, a little
pointedly, he changed the subject.

Honey Smith was the type of man whom everybody jokes, partly because he received it with
such good humor, partly because he turned it back
with so ready and so charming a wit. Also it gave
his fellow creatures a gratifying sense of equality
to pick humorous flaws in one so manifestly a
darling of the gods.

Honey Smith possessed not a trace of genius, not
a suggestion of what is popularly termed "temperament." He had no mind to speak of, and not
more than the usual amount of character. In fact,

but for one thing, he was an average person. That one thing was personality—and personality he possessed to an extraordinary degree. Indeed, there seemed to be something mysteriously compelling about this personality of Honey's. The whole world of creatures felt its charm. Dumb beasts fawned on him. Children clung to him. Old people lingered near as though they could light dead fires in the blaze of his radiant youth. Men hobnobbed with him; his charm brushed off on to the dryest and dullest so that, temporarily, they too bloomed with personality. As for women——His appearance among them was the signal for a noiseless social cataclysm. They slipped and slid in his direction as helplessly as if an inclined plane had opened under their feet. They fluttered in circles about him like birds around a light. If he had been allowed to follow the pull of his inclination, they would have held a subsidiary place in his existence. For he was practical, balanced, sane. He had, moreover, the tendency towards temperance of the born athlete. Besides all this, his main interests were man-interests. But women would not let him alone. He had but to look and the thing was done. Wreaths hung on every balcony for Honey Smith and, always at his approach, the door of the harem swung wide. He was a little lazy, almost discourteously uninterested in his attitude towards the individual female; for he had never had to exert himself.

It is likely that all this personal popularity would have been the result of that trick of personality. But many good fairies had been summoned to Honey's christening; he had good looks besides. He was really tall, although his broad shoulders seemed to reduce him to medium height. Brown-skinned, brown-eyed, brown-haired, his skin was as smooth as satin, his eyes as clear as crystal, his hair as thick as fur. His expression had tremendous sparkle. But his main physical charm was a smile which crumpled his brown face into an engaging irregularity of contour and lighted it with an expression brilliant with mirth and friendliness.

He was a true soldier of fortune. In the ten years which his business career covered he had engaged in a score of business ventures. He had lost two fortunes. Born in the West, educated in the East, he had flashed from coast to coast so often that he himself would have found it hard to say where he belonged.

He was the admiration and the wonder and the paragon and the criterion of his friend Billy Fairfax, who had trailed his meteoric course through college and who, when the *Brian Boru* went down, was accompanying him on his most recent adventure—a globe-trotting trip in the interests of a moving-picture company. Socially they made an excellent team. For Billy contributed money, birth, breeding, and position to augment Honey's initiative, enterprise, audacity, and charm. Billy Fairfax offered other contrasts quite as striking. On his physical side, he was shapelessly strong and hopelessly ugly, a big, shock-headed blond. On his personal side " mere mutt-man " was the way one girl put it, " too much of a damned gentleman " Honey Smith said to him regularly.

Billy Fairfax was not, however, without charm of a certain shy, evasive, slow-going kind; and he was not without his own distinction. His huge fortune had permitted him to cultivate many expensive sports and sporting tastes. His studs and kennels and strings of polo ponies were famous. He was a polo-player well above the average and an aviator not far below it.

Pete Murphy, the fifth of the group, was the delight of them all. The carriage of a bantam rooster, the courage of a lion, more brain than he could stagger under; a disposition fiery, mercurial, sanguine, witty; he was made, according to Billy Fairfax's dictum, of " wire and brass tacks," and he possessed what Honey Smith (who himself had no mean gift in that direction) called " the gift of gab." He lived by writing magazine articles. Also he wrote fiction, verse, and drama. Also he was a painter. Also he was a musician. In short, he was an Irishman.

Artistically, he had all the perception of the Celt plus the acquired sapience of the painter's training. If he could have existed in a universe which consisted entirely of sound and color, a universe inhabited only by disembodied spirits, he would have been its ablest citizen; but he was utterly disqualified to live in a human world. He was absolutely incapable of judging people. His tendency was to underestimate men and to overestimate women. His life bore all the scars inevitable to such an instinct. Women, in particular, had played ducks and drakes with his career. Weakly chivalrous, mindlessly gallant, he lacked the faculty of learning by experience—especially where the other sex were concerned. "Predestined to be stung!" was his first wife's laconic comment on her ex-husband. She, for instance, was undoubtedly the blameworthy one in their marital failure, but she had managed to extract a ruinous alimony from him. Twice married and twice divorced, he was traveling through the Orient to write a series of muckraking articles and, incidentally if possible, to forget his last unhappy matrimonial venture.

Physically, Pete was the black type of Celt. The wild thatch of his scrubbing-brush hair shone purple in the light. Scrape his face as he would, the purple shadow of his beard seemed ingrained in his white skin. Black-browed and black-lashed, he had the luminous blue-gray-green eyes of the colleen. There was a curious untamable quality in his look that was the mixture of two mad strains, the aloofness of the Celt and the aloofness of the genius.

Three weeks passed. The clear, warm-cool, lucid, sunny weather kept up. The ocean flattened gradually. Twice every twenty-four hours the tide brought treasure; but it brought less and less every day. Occasionally came a stiffened human reminder of their great disaster. But calloused as they were now to these experiences, the men buried it with hasty ceremony and forgot.

By this time an incongruous collection stretched in parallel lines above the high-water mark. "Something, anything, everything—and then some," remarked Honey Smith. Wood wreckage of all descriptions, acres of furniture, broken, split, blistered, discolored, swollen; piles of carpets, rugs, towels, bed-linen, stained, faded, shrunken, torn; files of swollen mattresses, pillows, cushions, life-preservers; heaps of table-silver and kitchen-ware tarnished and rusty; mounds of china and glass; mountains of tinned goods, barrels boxes, books, suit-cases, leather bags; trunks and trunks and more trunks and still more trunks; for, mainly, the trunks had saved themselves.

Part of the time, in between tides, they tried to separate the grain of this huge collection of lumber from the chaff; part of the time they made exploring trips into the interior. At night they sat about their huge fire and talked.

The island proved to be about twenty miles in length by seven in width. It was uninhabited and there were no large animals on it. It was Frank Merrill's theory that it was the exposed peak of a huge extinct volcano. In the center, filling the crater, was a little fresh-water lake. The island was heavily wooded; but in contour it presented only diminutive contrasts of hill and valley. And except as the semi-tropical foliage offered novelties of leaf and flower, the beauties of unfamiliar shapes and colors, it did not seem particularly interesting. Ralph Addington was the guide of these expeditions. From this tree, he pointed out, the South Sea Islander manufactured the tappa cloth, from that the poeepooee, from yonder the arva. Honey Smith used to say that the only depressing thing about these trips was the utter silence of the gorgeous birds which they saw on every side. On the other hand, they extracted what comfort they could from Merrill's and Addington's assurance that, should the ship's supply give out, they could live comfortably enough on birds' eggs, fruit, and fish.

Sorting what Honey Smith called the "ship-duffle" was one prolonged adventure. At first they made little progress; for all five of them gathered over each important find, chattering like girls. Each man followed the bent of his individual instinct for acquisitiveness. Frank Merrill picked out books, paper, writing materials of every sort. Ralph Addington ran to clothes. The habit of the man with whom it is a business policy to appear well-dressed maintained itself; even in their Eveless Eden, he presented a certain tailored smartness. Billy Fairfax selected kitchen utensils and tools. Later, he came across a box filled with tennis rackets, nets, and balls. The rackets' strings had

snapped and the balls were dead. He began immediately to restring the rackets, to make new balls
from twine, to lay out a court. Like true soldiers
of fortune, Honey Smith and Pete Murphy made
no special collection; they looted for mere loot's
sake.

One day, in the midst of one of their raids,
Honey Smith yelled a surprised and triumphant,
" By jiminy! " The others showed no signs of
interest. Honey was an alarmist; the treasure of
the moment might prove to be a Japanese print or
a corkscrew. But as nobody stirred or spoke, he
called, " The Wilmington ' Blue '! "

These words carried their inevitable magic. His
companions dropped everything; they swarmed
about him.

Honey held on his palm what, in the brilliant
sunlight looked like a globe of blue fire, a fire that
emitted rainbows instead of sparks.

He passed it from hand to hand. It seemed a
miracle that the fingers which touched it did not
burst into flame. For a moment the five men might
have been five children.

"Well," said Pete Murphy, "according to all fiction precedent, the rest of us ought to get together immediately, if not a little sooner, and murder you, Honey."

"Go as far as you like," said Honey, dropping the stone into the pocket of his flannel shirt. "Only if anybody really gets peeved about this junk of carbon, I'll give it to him."

For a while life flowed wonderful. The men labored with a joy-in-work at which they themselves marveled. Their out-of-doors existence showed its effects in a condition of glowing health. Honey Smith changed first to a brilliant red, then to a uniform coffee brown, and last to a shining bronze which was the mixture of both these colors. Pete Murphy grew one crop of freckles, then another and still another until Honey offered to "excavate" his features. Ralph Addington developed a rich, subcutaneous, golden-umber glow which made him seem, in connection with an occasional unconventionality of costume, more than ever like the schoolgirl's idea of an artist. Billy Fairfax's blond hair bleached to flaxen. His complexion deepened in tone to a permanent pink. This, in contrast with the deep clear blue of his eyes, gave him a kind of out-of-doors comeliness. But Frank Merrill was the surprise of them all. He not only grew handsomer, he grew younger; a magnificent, towering, copper-colored monolith of a man, whose gray eyes were as clear as mountain springs, whose white teeth turned his smile to a flash of light. Constantly they patrolled the beach, pairs of them, studying the ocean for sight of a distant sail, selecting at intervals a new spot on which at night to start fires, or by day to erect signals. They bubbled with spirits. They laughed and talked without cessation. The condition which Ralph Addington had deplored, the absence of women, made at first for social relaxation, for psychological rest.

" Lord, I never noticed before—until I got this chance to get off and think of it—what a damned bother women are," Honey Smith said one day. " Of all the sexes that roam the earth, as George Ade says, I like them least. What a mess they make of your time and your work, always requiring so much attention, always having to be waited on, always dropping things, always so much foolish fuss and ceremony, always asking such footless questions and never hearing you when you answer them. Never really knowing anything or saying anything. They're a different kind of critter, that's all there is to it; they're amateurs at life. They're a failure as a sex and an outworn convention anyway. Myself, I'm for sending them to the scrap-heap. Votes for men!"

And with this, according to the divagations of their temperaments and characters, the others strenuously concurred.

Their days, crowded to the brim with work, passed so swiftly that they scarcely noticed their flight. Their nights, filled with a sleep that was twin brother to Death, seemed not to exist at all.

Their evenings were lively with the most brilliant kind of man-talk. To it, Frank Merrill brought his encyclopedic book knowledge, his insatiable curiosity about life; Ralph Addington all the garnered richness of his acute observation; Billy Fairfax his acquaintance with the elect of the society or of the art world, his quiet, deferential attitude of listener. But the events of these conversational orgies were Honey Smith's adventures and Pete Murphy's romances. Honey's narrative was crisp, clear, quick, straight from the shoulder, colloquial, slangy. He dealt often in the first person and the present tense. He told a plain tale from its simple beginning to its simple end. But Pete—— His language had all Honey's simplicity and terseness and, in addition, he had the literary touch, both the dramatist's instinct and the fictionist's insight. His stories always ran up to a psychological climax; but this was always disguised by the best narratory tricks. He was one of those men of whom people always say, "if he could only write as he talks." In point of fact, he wrote much better than he talked—but he talked better than any one else. The unanalytic never allowed in him for the spell of the spoken word, nor for the fiery quality of his spirit.

As time went on, their talks grew more and more confidential. Women's faces began to gleam here and there in narrative. They began to indulge in long discussions of the despised sex; at

times they ran into fierce controversy. Occasionally Honey Smith re-told a story which, from the
introduction of a shadowy girl-figure, became mysteriously more interesting and compelling. Once
or twice they nearly went over the border-line of
legitimate confidence, so intimate had their talk become—muffled as it was by the velvety, star-sown
dark and interrupted only by the unheeded thun-
ders of the surf. They were always pulling themselves up to debate openly whether they should go
farther, always, on consideration, turning narrative
into a channel much less confidential and much less
interesting, or as openly plugging straight ahead,
carefully disguising names and places.

After a week or two, the first fine careless rapture of their escape from death disappeared. The
lure of loot evaporated. They did not stop their
work on " the ship-duffle," but it became aimless
and undirected. Their trips into the island seemed
a little purposeless. Frank Merrill had to scourge
them to patrol the beach, to keep their signal
sheets flying, their signal fires burning. The
effect upon their mental condition of this loss

of animus was immediate. They became perceptibly more serious. Their first camp—it consisted
only of five haphazard piles of bedding—satisfied
superficially the shiftless habits of their womanless
group; subconsciously, however, they all fell under
the depression of its discomfort and disorder.
They bathed in the ocean regularly but they did
not shave. Their clothes grew ragged and torn,
and although there were scores of trunks packed
with wearing apparel, they did not bother to
change them. Subconsciously they all responded
to these irregularities by a sudden change in spirit.

In the place of the gay talk-fests that filled their
evenings, they began to hold long pessimistic discussions about their future on the island in case
rescue were indefinitely delayed. Taciturn periods
fell upon them. Frank Merrill showed only a
slight seriousness. Billy Fairfax, however, wore a
look permanently sobered. Pete Murphy became
subject at regular intervals to wild rhapsodical sei-
zures when he raved, almost in impromptu verse,
about the beauty of sea and sky. These were followed by periods of an intense, bitter, black, Celtic

melancholy. Ralph Addington degenerated into what Honey described as "the human sourball." He spoke as seldom as possible and then only to snarl. He showed a tendency to disobey the few orders that Frank Merrill, who still held his position of leader, laid upon them. Once or twice he grazed a quarrel with Merrill. Honey Smith developed an abnormality equal to Ralph Addington's, but in the opposite direction. His spirits never flagged; he brimmed with joy-in-life, vitality, and optimism. It was as if he had some secret mental solace.

"Damn you and your sunny-side-up dope!" Ralph Addington growled at him again and again. "Shut up, will you!"

One day Frank Merrill proposed a hike across the island. Billy Fairfax who, at the head, had set a brisk pace for the file, suddenly dropped back to the rear and accosted Honey Smith who had lagged behind. Honey was skipping stones over the lake from a pocketful of flat pebbles.

"Say, Honey," Billy began. The other four men were far ahead, but Billy kept his voice low.

" Do you remember that dream you had about the big bird—the time we joshed you so? "

" Sure do I," Honey said cheerfully. " Only remember one thing, Billy. That wasn't a dream any more than this is."

" All right," Billy exclaimed. " You don't have to show me. A funny thing happened to me last night. I'm not telling the others. They won't believe it and—well, my nerves are all on end. I know I'd get mad if they began to jolly. I was sleeping like the dickens—a sure-for-certain Rip Van Winkle—when all of a sudden—— Did you ever have a pet cat, Honey? "

" Nope."

" Well, I've had lots of them. I like cats. I had one once that used to wake me up at two minutes past seven every morning as regularly as two minutes past seven came—not an instant before, not an instant after. He turned the trick by jumping up on the bed and looking steadily into my face. Never touched me, you understand. Well, I waked this morning just after sunrise with a feeling that Kilo was there staring at me. Somebody was—"

Billy paused. He swallowed rapidly and wet his lips. " But it wasn't Kilo." Billy paused again.

" I'm listening, bo," said Honey, shying another stone.

" It was a girl looking at me," Billy said, simply as though it were something to be expected. He paused. Then, " Get that? A *girl!* She was bending over me—pretty close—I could almost touch her. I can see her now as plainly as I see you. She was blonde. One of those pale-gold blondes with hair like honey and features cut with a chisel. You know the type. Some people think it's cold. It's a kind of beauty that's always appealed to me, though." He stopped.

" Well," Honey prodded him with a kind of non-committal calm, " what happened? "

" Nothing. If you can believe me—*nothing*. I stared—oh, I guess I stared for a quarter of a minute—straight up into the most beautiful pair of eyes that I ever saw in my life. I stared straight *up* into them and I stared straight *down* into them. They were as deep as a well and as gray as a cloud and as cold as ice. And they had lashes——"

For a moment the quiet directness of Billy's narrative was disturbed by a whiff of inner tumult. "Whew! what eyelashes! Honey, did you ever come across a lonely mountain lake with high reeds growing around the edge? You know how pure and unspoiled and virginal it seems. That was her eyes. They sort of hypnotized me. My eyes closed and—when I awoke it was broad daylight. What do you think?"

"Well," said Honey judicially, "I know just how you feel. I could have killed the boys for joshing me the way they did. I was sure. I was certain I heard a woman laugh that night. And, by God, I did hear it. Whenever I contradict myself, something rises up and tells me I lie. But——" His radiant brown smile crumpled his brown face. "Of course, I *didn't* hear it. I *couldn't* have heard it. And so I guess you didn't see the peroxide you speak of. And yet if you punch me in the jaw, I'll know exactly how you feel." His face uncrumpled, smoothed itself out to his rare look of seriousness. "The point of it is that we're all a little touched in the bean. I figure that you and I are alike in some things. That's why we've always hung together. And all this queer stuff takes us two the same way. Remember that psychology dope old Rand used to pump into us at college? Well, our psychologies have got all twisted up by a recent event in nautical circles and we're seeing things that *aren't* there and not seeing things that *are* there."

"Honey," said Billy, "that's all right. But I want you to understand me and I don't want you to make any mistake. I *saw* a girl."

"And don't forget this," answered Honey. "I *heard* one."

Billy made no allusion to any of this with the other three men. But for the rest of the day, he had a return of his gentle good humor. Honey's spirits fairly sizzled.

That night Frank Merrill suddenly started out of sleep with a yelled, "What was that?"

"What was what?" everybody demanded, waking immediately to the panic in his voice.

"That cry," he explained breathlessly, "didn't

you hear it?" Frank's eyes were brilliant with excitement; he was pale.

Nobody had heard it. And Ralph Addington and Pete Murphy, cursing lustily, turned over and promptly fell asleep again. But Billy Fairfax grew rapidly more and more awake. "What sort of a cry?" he asked. Honey Smith said nothing, but he stirred the fire into a blaze in preparation for a talk.

"The strangest cry I ever heard, long-drawn-out, wild—eerie's the word for it, I guess," Frank Merrill said. As he spoke, he peered off into the darkness. "If it were possible, I should say it was a woman's voice."

The three men walked away from the camp, looked off into every direction of the starlit night. Nowhere was there sign or sound of life.

"It must have been gulls," said Honey Smith.

"It didn't sound like gulls," answered Frank Merrill. For an instant he fell into meditation so deep that he virtually forgot the presence of the other two. "I don't know what it was," he said finally in an exasperated tone. "I'm going to sleep."

They walked back to camp. Frank Merrill rolled himself up in a blanket, lay down. Soon there came from his direction only the sound of regular, deep breathing.

"Well, Honey," Billy Fairfax asked, a note of triumph in his voice, "how about it?"

"Well, Billy," Honey Smith said in a baffled tone, "when you get the answer, give it to me."

Nobody mentioned the night's experience the next day. But a dozen times Frank Merrill stopped his work to gaze out to sea, an expression of perplexity on his face.

The next night, however, they were all waked again, waked twice. It was Ralph Addington who spoke first; a kind of hoarse grunt and a "What the devil was that?"

"What?" the others called.

"Damned if I know," Ralph answered. "If you wouldn't think I was off my conch, I'd say it was a gang of women laughing."

Pete Murphy, who always woke in high spirits,

began to joke Ralph Addington. The other three were silent. In fifteen minutes they were all asleep; in sixty, they were all awake again.

It was Pete Murphy who sounded the alarm this time. "Say, something spoke to me," he said. "Or else I'm a nut. Or else I have had the most vivid dream I've ever had." Evidently he did not believe that it was a dream. He sat up and listened; the others listened, too. There was no sound in the soft, still night, however. They talked for a little while, a strangely subdued quintette. It was as though they were all trying to comment on these experiences without saying anything about them.

They slept through the next night undisturbed until just before sunrise. Then Honey Smith woke them. It was still dark, but a fine dawn-glow had begun faintly to silver the east. "Say, you fellows," he exclaimed. "Wake up!" His voice vibrated with excitement, although he seemed to try to keep it low. "There are strange critters round here. No mistake this time. Woke with a start, feeling that something had brushed over me

—saw a great bird—a gigantic thing—flying off—heard one woman's laugh—then another——"

It was significant that nobody joked Honey this time. " Say, this island'll be a nut-house if this keeps up," Pete Murphy said irritably. " Let's go to sleep again."

" No, you don't! " said Honey. " Not one of you is going to sleep. You're all going to sit up with me until the blasted sun comes up."

People always hastened to accommodate Honey. In spite of the hour, they began to rake the fire, to prepare breakfast. The others became preoccupied gradually, but Honey still sat with his face towards the water, watching.

It grew brighter.

" It's time we started to build a camp, boys," Frank Merrill said, withdrawing momentarily from deep reflection. " We'll go crazy doing nothing all the time. We'll——"

" Great God," Honey interrupted. " Look! "

Far out to sea and high in the air, birds were flying. There were five of them and they were enormous. They flew with amazing strength,

swiftness, and grace; but for the most part they
buzzed about a fixed area like bees at a honey-
pot. It was a limited area, but within it
they dipped, dropped, curved, wove in and
out.

"Well, I'll be——"

"They're those black spots we saw the first
day, Pete," Billy Fairfax said breathlessly. "We
thought it was the sun."

"That's what I heard in the night," Frank Merrill gasped to Ralph Addington.

"But what are they?" asked Honey Smith in
a voice that had a falsetto note of wonder. "They
laugh like a woman—take it from me."

"Eagles—buzzards—vultures—condors—rocs
—phœnixes," Pete Murphy recited his list in an
orgy of imaginative conjecture.

"They're some lost species—something left over
from a prehistoric era," Frank Merrill explained,
shaking with excitement. "No vulture or eagle
or condor could be as big as that at this distance.
At least I think so." He paused here, as one studying the problem in the scientific spirit. "Often in

the Rockies I've confused a nearby chicken-hawk, at first, with a far eagle. But the human eye has its own system of triangulation. Those are not little birds nearby, but big birds far off. See how heavily they soar. Do you realize what's happened? We've made a discovery that will shake the whole scientific world. There, there, they're going!"

"My God, look at them beat it!" said Honey; and there was awe in his voice.

"Why, they're monster size," Frank Merrill went on, and his voice had grown almost hysterical. "They could carry one of us off. We're not safe. We must take measures at once to protect ourselves. Why, at night—— We must make traps. If we can capture one, or, better, a pair, we're famous. We're a part of history now."

They watched the strange birds disappear over the water. For more than an hour, the men sat still, waiting for them to return. They did not come back, however. The men hung about camp all day long, talking of nothing else. Night came at last, but sleep was not in them. The dark seemed to give a fresh impulse to conversation. Conjecture battled with theory and fact jousted with fancy. But one conclusion was as futile as another.

Frank Merrill tried to make them devise some system of defense or concealment, but the others laughed at him. Talk as he would, he could not seem to convince them of their danger. Indeed, their state of mind was entirely different from his. Mentally he seemed to boil with interest and curiosity, but it was the sane, calm, open-minded excitement of the scientist. The others were alert and preoccupied in turn, but there was an element of reserve in their attitude. Their eyes kept going off into space, fixing there until their look became one brooding question. They avoided conversation. They avoided each other's gaze.

Gradually they drew off from the fire, settled themselves to rest, fell into the splendid sleep that followed their long out-of-doors days.

In the middle of the night, Billy Fairfax came out of a dream to the knowledge that somebody was shaking him gently, firmly, furtively. " Don't move!" Honey Smith's voice whispered; "keep quiet till I wake the others."

It was a still and moon-lighted world. Billy Fairfax lay quiet, his wide-open eyes fixed on the luminous sky. The sense of drowse was being brushed out of his brain as though by a mighty whirlwind, and in its place came a vague sensation of confusion, of excitement, of a miraculous abnormality. He heard Honey Smith crawl slowly from man to man, heard him whisper his adjuration once, twice, three times. "Now," Honey called finally.

The men looked seawards. Then, simultaneously they leaped to their feet.

The semi-tropical moon was at its full. Huge, white, embossed, cut out, it did not shine—it glared from the sky. It made a melted moonstone of the atmosphere. It faded the few clouds to a sapphire-gray, just touched here and there with the chalky dot of a star. It slashed a silver trail across a sea jet-black except where the waves rimmed it with snow. Up in the white enchantment, but not far above them, the strange air-creatures were fly-

ing. They were not birds; they were winged
women!

Darting, diving, glancing, curving, wheeling,
they interwove in what seemed the premeditated
figures of an aerial dance. If they were conscious
of the group of men on the beach, they did not
show it; they seemed entirely absorbed in their flying. Their wings, like enormous scimitars, caught
the moonlight, flashed it back. For an interval,
they played close in a group inextricably intertwined, a revolving ball of vivid color. Then, as
if seized by a common impulse, they stretched,
hand in hand, in a line across the sky—drifted.
The moonlight flooded them full, caught glitter
and gleam from wing-sockets, shot shimmer and
sheen from wing-tips, sent cataracts of iridescent
color pulsing between. Snow-silver one, brilliant
green and gold another, dazzling blue the next,
luminous orange a fourth, flaming flamingo scarlet
the last, their colors seemed half liquid, half light.
One moment the whole figure would flare into a
splendid blaze, as if an inner mechanism had suddenly turned on all the electricity; the next, the

blaze died down to the fairy glisten given by the moonlight.

As if by one impulse, they began finally to fly upward. Higher and higher they rose, still hand in hand. Detail of color and movement vanished. The connotation of the sexed creature, of the human thing, evaporated. One instant, relaxed, they seemed tiny galleons, all sails set, that floated lazily, the sport of an aerial sea; another, supple and sinuous, they seemed monstrous fish whose fins triumphantly clove the air, monarchs of that aerial sea.

A little of this and then came another impulse. The great wings furled close like blades leaping back to scabbard; the flying-girls dropped sheer in a dizzying fall. Half-way to the ground, they stopped simultaneously as if caught by some invisible air plateau. The great feathery fans opened —and this time the men got the whipping whirr of them—spread high, palpitated with color. From this lower level, the girls began to fall again, but gently, like dropping clouds.

Nearer they came to the petrified group on the

beach, nearer and nearer. Undoubtedly they had known all the time that an audience was there; undoubtedly they had planned this; they looked down and smiled.

And now the men had every detail of them—the brown seaweeds and green sea-grasses that swathed them, their bodies just short of heroic size, deep-bosomed, broad-waisted, long-limbed; their arms round like a woman's and strong like a man's; their hair that fell, a braid over each ear, twined with brilliant flowers and green vines; their faces super-humanly beautiful, though elvish; the *gaminerie* in their laughing eyes, which sparkled through half-closed, thick-lashed lids, the *gaminerie* in their smiling mouths, which showed twin rows of pearl gleaming in tricksy mirth; their big, strong-look-ing, long-fingered hands; their slimly smooth, ex-quisitely shaped, too-tiny, transparent feet; their strong wrists; their stem-like, breakable ankles. Closer and closer and closer they came. And now the men could almost touch them. They paused an instant and fluttered—fluttered like a swarm of butterflies undecided where to fly. As though choosing to rest, they hovered—hovered with a gentle, slow, seductive undulation of wings, of hands, of feet.

Then another impulse took them.

They broke handclasps and up they went, like arrows straight up—up—up—up. Then they turned out to sea, streaming through the air in line still, but one behind the other. And for the first time, sound came from them; they threw off peals of girl-laughter that fell like handfuls of diamonds. Their mirth ended in a long, eerie cry. Then straight out to the eastern horizon they went and away and off.

They were dwindling rapidly.

They were spots.

They were specks.

They were nothing.

II

SILENCE, profound, portentous, protracted, followed.

Finally, Honey Smith absently stooped and picked up a pebble. He threw it over the silver ring of the flat, foam-edged, low-tide waves. It curved downwards, hissed across a surface of water smooth as jade, skipped four times, and dropped.

The men strained their eyes to follow the progress of this tangible thing.

" Where do you suppose they've gone? " Honey said as unexcitedly as one might inquire directions from a stranger.

" When do you suppose they'll come back? " Billy Fairfax added as casually as one might ask the time.

" Did you notice the red-headed one? " asked Pete Murphy. " My first girl had red hair. I always jump when I see a carrot-top." He made this intimate revelation simply, as if the time for a conventional reticence had passed.

"They were lookers all right," Ralph Addington went on. "I'd pick the golden blonde, the second from the right." He, too, spoke in a matter-of-fact tone, as though he were selecting a favorite from the front row in the chorus.

"It must have happened if we saw it," Frank Merrill said. There was in his voice a note of petulance, almost childish. "But we ought not to have seen it. It has no right to be. It upsets things so."

"What are we all standing up like gawks for?" Pete Murphy demanded with a sudden irritability. "Sit down!"

Everybody dropped. They all sat as they fell. They sat motionless. They sat silent.

"The name of this place is 'Angel Island,'" announced Billy Fairfax after a long time. His tone was that of a man whose thoughts, swirling in phantasmagoria, seek anchorage in fact.

They did not sleep that night.

When Frank Merrill arose the next morning, Ralph Addington was just returning from a stroll down the beach. Ralph looked at the same time exhausted and recuperated. He was white, tense, wild-eyed, but recently aroused interior fires glowed through his skin, made up for his lost color and energy. Frank also had a different look. His eyes had kindled, his face had become noticeably more alive. But it was the fire of the intellect that had produced this frigid glow.

"Seen anything?" Frank Merrill inquired.

"Not a thing."

"You don't think they're frightened enough not to come back?"

The gleam in Ralph Addington's eye changed to flame. "I don't think they're frightened at all. They'll come back all right. There's only one thing that you can depend on in women; and that is that you can't lose them."

"I can scarcely wait to see them again," Frank exclaimed eagerly. "Addington, I can write a monograph on those flying-maidens that will make the whole world gasp. This is the greatest discovery of modern times. Man alive, don't you itch to get to paper and pencil?"

"Not so I've noticed it," Ralph replied with contemptuous emphasis. "I shall lie awake nights, just the same though."

"Say, fellers, we didn't dream that, did we?" Billy Fairfax called suddenly, rolling out of the sleep that had followed their all-night talk.

"Well, I reckon if it wasn't for the other four, no one of us would trust his own senses," Frank Merrill said dryly.

"If you'd listened to me in the beginning," Honey Smith remarked in a drowsy voice, not bothering to open his eyes, "I wouldn't be the I-told-you-so kid now."

"Well, if you'd listened to me and Pete!" said Billy Fairfax; "didn't we think, way back there that first day, that our lamps were on the blink because we saw black spots? Great Scott, what dreams I've had," he went on, "a mixture of 'Arabian Nights,' 'Gulliver's Travels,' 'Peter Wilkins,' 'Peter Pan,' 'Goosie,' Jules Verne, H.

G. Wells, and every dime novel I've ever read.
Do you suppose they'll come back?"

"I've just talked that over with Ralph," Frank
Merrill answered him. "If we've frightened them
away forever, it will be a terrible loss to science."

Ralph Addington emitted one of his cackling,
ironic laughs. "I guess I'm not worrying as much
about science as I might. But as to their coming
back—why, it stands to reason that they'll have
just as much curiosity about us as we have about
them. Curiosity's a woman's strong point, you
know. Oh, they'll come back all right! The only
question is, How soon?"

"It made me dream of music—of Siegfried."
It was Pete Murphy who spoke and he seemed to
plump from sleep straight into the conversation.
"What a theme for grand opera. Women with
wings! Flying-girls! Will you tell me what the
Hippodrome has on Angel Island?"

"Nothing," said Honey Smith, "except this—
you *can* get acquainted with a Hippodrome girl—
how long is it going to take us to get acquainted
with these angels?"

"Not any longer than usual," said Ralph Addington with an expressive wink. "Leave that to me. I'm going now to see what I can see." He walked rapidly down the beach, scaled the southern reef, and stood there studying the horizon.

The others remained sitting on the sand. For a while they watched Ralph. Then they talked the whole thing over with as much interest as if they had not yet discussed it. Ralph rejoined them and they went through it again. It was as though by some miracle of mind-transference, they had all dreamed the same dream; as though, by some miracle of sight-transference they had all seen the same vision; as though, by some miracle of space-transference, they had all stepped into the fourth dimension. Their comment was ever of the wonder of their strange adventure, the beauty, the thrill, the romance of it. It had brought out in them every instinct of chivalry and kindness, it had developed in them every tendency towards high-mindedness and idealism. Angel Island would be an Atlantis, an Eden,

an Arden, an Arcadia, a Utopia, a Mille-
amours, a Paradise, the Garden of Hesperides.
Into it the Golden Age would come again. They
drew glowing pictures of the wonderful friend-
ships that would grow up on Angel Island between
them and their beautiful visitors. These poetic
considerations gave way finally to a discussion of
ways and means. They agreed that they must get
to work at once on some sort of shelter for their
guests, in case the weather should turn bad. They
even discussed at length the best methods of teach-
ing the English language. They talked the whole
morning, going over the same things again and
again, questioning each other eagerly without
listening for an answer, interrupting ruthlessly,
and then adding nothing.

The day passed without event. At the slightest
sound they all jumped. Their sleeplessness was
beginning to tell on them and their nerves were
still obsessed by the unnaturalness of their experience. It was a long time before they quieted down,
but the night passed without interruption. So did
the next day. Another day went by and another,

and during this time they did little but sit about and talk.

"See here, boys," Ralph Addington said one morning. "I say we get together and build some cabins. There's no calculating how long this grand weather'll keep up. The first thing we know we'll be up against a rainy season. Isn't that right, Professor?"

On most practical matters Ralph treated Frank Merrill's opinion with a contempt that was offensively obvious to the others. In questions of theory or of abstruse information, he was foolishly deferential. At those times, he always gave Frank his title of Professor.

"I hardly think so," Frank Merrill answered. "I think we'll have an equable, semi-tropical climate all the year round—about like Honolulu."

"Well, anyway," Ralph Addington went on, "it's barbarous living like this. And we want to be prepared for anything." His gaze left Frank Merrill's face and traveled with a growing significance to each of the other three. "*Anything*," he repeated with emphasis. "We've got enough

truck here to make a young Buckingham Palace.
And we'll go mad sitting round waiting for those
air-queens to pay us a visit. How about it?"

"It's an excellent idea," Frank Merrill said
heartily. "I have been on the point of proposing
it many times myself."

However, they seemed unable to pull themselves
together; they did nothing that day. But the next
morning, urged back to work by the harrying
monotony of waiting, they began to clear a space
among the trees close to the beach. Two of them
had a little practical building knowledge: Ralph
Addington who had roughed it in many strange
countries; Billy Fairfax who, in the San Francisco
earthquake, had on a wager built himself a house.
They worked with all their initial energy. They
worked with the impetus that comes from capable
supervision. And they worked as if under the impulse of some unformulated motive. As usual,
Honey Smith bubbled with spirits. Billy Fairfax and Pete Murphy hardly spoke, so close was
their concentration. Ralph Addington worked
longer and harder than anybody, and even Honey

was not more gay; he whistled and sang constantly. Frank Merrill showed no real interest in these proceedings. He did his fair share of the work, but obviously without a driving motive. He had reverted utterly to type. He spent his leisure writing a monograph. When inspiration ran low, he occupied himself doctoring books. Eternally, he hunted for the flat stones between which he pressed their swollen bulks back to shape. Eternally he puttered about, mending and patching them. He used to sit for hours at a desk which he had rescued from the ship's furniture. The others never became accustomed to the comic incongruity of this picture—especially when, later, he virtually boxed himself in with a trio of book-cases.

"Wouldn't you think he was sitting in an office?" Ralph Addington said.

"Curious about Merrill," Honey Smith answered, indulging in one of his sudden, off-hand characterizations, bull's-eye shots every one of them. "He's a good man, ruined by culturine. He's the bucko-mate type translated into the language of the academic world. Three centuries ago he'd have been a Drake or a Frobisher. And to-day, even, if he'd followed the lead of his real ability, he'd have made a great financier, a captain of industry or a party boss. But, you see, he was brought up to think that book-education was the whole cheese. The only ambition he knows is to make good in the university world. How I hated that college atmosphere and its insistence on culture! That was what riled me most about it. As a general thing, I detest a professor. Can't help liking old Frank, though."

The four men virtually took no time off from work; or at least the change of work that stood for leisure was all in the line of home-making. Eternally, they joked each other about these womanish occupations; but they all kept steadily to it. Ralph Addington and Honey Smith put the furniture into shape, repairing and polishing it. Billy Fairfax sorted out the glass, china, tools, household utensils of every kind.

Pete Murphy went through the trunks with his art side uppermost. He collected all kinds of Oriental bric-à-brac, pictures and draperies. He actually mended and pressed things; he had all the artist's capability in these various feminine lines. When the others joked him about his exotic and impracticable tastes, he said that, before he left, he intended to establish a museum of fine arts on Angel Island.

Hard as the men worked, they had always the appearance of those who await the expected. But the expected did not occur; and gradually the sharp edge of anticipation wore dull. Emotionally they calmed. Their nerves settled to a normal condition. The sudden whirr of a bird's flight attracted only a casual glance. In Ralph Addington alone, expectation maintained itself at the boiling point. He trained himself to work with one eye searching the horizon. One afternoon, when they had scattered for a siesta, his hoarse cry brought them running to the beach from all directions.

So suddenly had the girls appeared that they might have materialized from the air. This time they had not come from the sea. When Ralph discovered them, they were hovering back of them above the trees that banded the beach. The sun was setting, blood-red; the whole western sky had broken away. The girls seemed to be floating in a sea of crimson-amber ether. Its light brought lustre to every feather; it turned the edges of their wings to flame; it changed their smoothly piled hair to helmets of burnished metal.

The men tore from the beach to the trees at full speed. For a moment the violence of this action threw the girls into a panic. They fluttered, broke lines, flew high, circled. And all the time, they uttered shrill cries of distress.

" They're frightened," Billy Fairfax said. " Keep quiet, boys."

The men stopped running, stood stock-still.

Gradually the girls calmed, sank, took up the interweaving figures of their air-dance. If at their first appearance they seemed creatures of the sea, this time they were as distinctively of the forest. They looked like spirits of the trees over which they hovered. Indeed, but for their wings they might have been dryads. Wreaths of green encircled their heads and waists. Long leafy streamers trailed from their shoulders. Often in the course of their aerial play, they plunged down into the feathery tree-tops.

Once, the blonde with the blue wings sailed out of the group and balanced herself for a toppling second on a long, outstretching bough.

"Good Lord, what a picture!" Pete Murphy said.

As if she understood, she repeated her performance. She cast a glance over her shoulder at them —unmistakably noting the effect.

"Hates herself, doesn't she?" commented Honey Smith. "They're talking!" he added after an interval of silence. "Some one of them is giving directions—I can tell by the tone of her voice. Can't make out which one it is though. Thank God, they can talk!"

"It's the quiet one—the blonde—the one with the white wings," Billy Fairfax explained. "She's captain. Some bean on her, too; she straightened them out a moment ago when they got so frightened."

"I now officially file my claim," said Ralph Ad-

dington, " to that peachy one—the golden blonde
—the one with the blue wings, the one who tried
to stand on the bough. That girl's a corker. I
can tell her kind of pirate craft as far as I
see it."

" Me for the thin one! " said Pete Murphy.
" She's a pippin, if you please. Quick as a cat!
Graceful as they make them. And look at that
mop of red hair! Isn't that a holocaust? I bet
she's a shrew."

" You win, all right," agreed Ralph Addington.
" I'd like nothing better than the job of taming
her, too."

" See here, Ralph," bantered Pete, " I've copped
Brick-top for myself. You keep off the grass.
See! "

" All right," Ralph answered. " Katherine for
yours, Petruchio. The golden blonde for mine! "
He smiled for the first time in days. In fact, at
sight of the flying-girls he had begun to beam with
fatuous good nature.

" Two blondes, two brunettes, and a red-top,"
said Honey Smith, summing them up practically.

"One of those brunettes, the brown one, must be a Kanaka. The other's prettier—she looks like a Spanish woman. There's something rather taking about the plain one, though. Pretty snappy—if anybody should fly up in a biplane and ask you!"

"It's curious," Frank Merrill said with his most academic manner, "it has not yet occurred to me to consider those young women from the point of view of their physical pulchritude. I'm interested only in their ability to fly. The one with the silver-white wings, the one Billy calls the 'quiet one,' flies better than any of the others. The dark one on the end, the one who looks like a Spaniard, flies least well. It is rather disturbing, but I can think of them only as birds. I have to keep recalling to myself that they're women. I can't realize it."

"Well, don't worry," Ralph Addington said with the contemptuous accent with which latterly he answered all Frank Merrill's remarks. "You will."

The others laughed, but Frank turned on them a look of severe reproof.

"Oh, hell!" Honey Smith exclaimed in a regretful tone; "they're beating it again. I say, girls," he called at the top of his lungs, "don't go! Stay a little longer and we'll buy you a dinner and a taxi-cab."

Apparently the flying-girls realized that he was addressing them. For a hair's breadth of a second they paused. Then, with a speed that had a suggestion of panic in it, they flew out to sea. And again a flood of girl-laughter fell in bubbles upon them.

"They distrust muh!" Honey commented. But he smiled with the indolent amusement of the man who has always held the master-hand with women.

"Must have come from the east, this time," he said as they filed soberly back to camp. "But where in thunder do they start from?"

They had, of course, discussed this question as they had discussed a hundred other obvious ones. "I'm wondering now," Frank Merrill answered, "if there are islands both to the east and the west. But, after all, I'm more interested to know if there are any more of these winged women, and if there are any males."

Again they talked far into the night. And as before their comment was of the wonder, the romance, the poetry of their strange situation. And again they drew imaginary pictures of what Honey Smith called "the young Golden Age" that they would soon institute on Angel Island.

"Say," Honey remarked facetiously when at length they started to run down, "what happens to a man if he marries an angel? Does he become angel-consort or one of those seraphim arrangements?"

Ralph Addington laughed. But Billy Fairfax and Pete Murphy frowned. Frank Merrill did not seem to hear him. He was taking notes by the firelight.

The men continued to work at the high rate of speed that, since the appearance of the women, they had set for themselves. But whatever form their labor took, their talk was ever of the flying-girls. They referred to them individually now as the "dark one," the "plain one," the "thin one," the

" quiet one," and the " peachy one." They theo-
rized eternally about them. It was a long time,
however, before they saw them again, so long that
they had begun to get impatient. In Ralph Addington this uneasiness took the form of irritation.
" If I'd had a gun," he snarled more than once,
" by the Lord Harry, I'd have winged one of
them." He sat far into the night and waited. He
arose early in the morning and watched. He went
for long, slow, solitary, silent, prowling hikes into
the interior. His eyes began to look strained from
so minute a study of the horizon-line. He grew
haggard. His attitude in the matter annoyed Pete
Murphy, who maintained that he had no right to
spy on women. Argument broke out between
them, waxing hot, waned to silence, broke out
again and with increased fury. Frank Merrill and
Billy Fairfax listened to all this, occasionally
smoothing things over between the disputants.
But Honey Smith, who seemed more amused than
bothered, deftly fed the flame of controversy by
agreeing first with one and then with the other.

Late one afternoon, just as the evening star

flashed the signal of twilight, the girls came streaming over the sea toward the island.

At the first far-away glimpse, the men dropped their tools and ran to the water's edge. Honey Smith waded out, waist-deep.

"Well, what do you know about that?" he called out. "Pipe the formation!"

They came massed vertically. In the distance they might have been a rainbow torn from its moorings, borne violently forward on a high wind. The rainbow broke in spots, fluttered, and then came together again. It vibrated with color. It pulsed with iridescence.

"How the thunder——" Addington began and stopped. "Well, can you beat it?" he concluded.

The human column was so arranged that the wings of one of the air-girls concealed the body of another just above her.

The "dark one" led, flying low, her scarlet pinions beating slowly back and forth about her head.

Just above, near enough for her body to be concealed by the scarlet wings of the " dark one," but high enough for her pointed brown face to peer between their curves, came the " plain one."

Higher flew the " thin one." Her body was entirely covered by the orange wings of the " plain one," but her copper-colored hair made a gleamy spot in their vase-shaped opening.

Still higher appeared the " peachy one." She seemed to be holding her lustrous blonde head carefully centered in the oval between the " thin one's " green-and-yellow plumage. She looked like a portrait in a frame.

Highest of them all, floating upright, a Winged Victory of the air, her silver wings towering straight above her head, the cameo face of the " quiet one " looked level into the distance.

Their wings moved in rotation, and with machine-like regularity. First one pair flashed up, swept back and down, then another and another. As they neared, the color seemed the least wonderful detail of the picture. For it changed in effect from a column of glittering wings to a column of girl-faces, a column that floated light as thistle-down, a column that divided, parted, opened, closed again.

The background of all this was a veil of dark gauze at the horizon-line, its foil a golden, virgin moon, dangling a single brilliant star.

" They're talking! " Honey Smith exclaimed. " And they're leaving! "

The girls did not pause once. They flew in a straight line over the island to the west, always maintaining their columnar formation. At first the men thought that they were making for the trees. They ran after them. The speed of their running had no effect this time on their visitors, who continued to sail eastward. The men called on them to stay. They called repeatedly, singly and in chorus. They called in every tone of humble masculine entreaty and of arrogant masculine command. But their cries might have fallen on marble ears. The girls neither turned nor paused. They disappeared.

" Females are certainly alike under their skins, whether they're angels or Hottentots," Ralph Addington commented. " That tableau appearance

was all cooked up for us. They must have prac-
tised it for hours."

"It has the rose-carnival at Tetaluma, Cal.,
faded," remarked Honey Smith.

"The 'quiet one' was giving the orders for
that wing-movement," said Billy Fairfax. "She
whispered them, but I heard her. She engineered
the whole thing. She seems to be their leader."

"I got their voices this time," said Pete Murphy. "Beautiful, all of them. Soprano, high and
clear. They've got a language, all right, too.
What did you think of it, Frank?"

"Most interesting," replied Frank Merrill,
"*most* interesting. A preponderance of conso-
nants. Never guttural in effect, and as you say,
beautiful voices, very high and clear."

"I don't see why they don't stop and play,"
complained Honey. His tone was the petulant
one of a spoiled child. It is likely that during the
whole course of his woman-petted existence, he
had never been so completely ignored. "If I
only knew their lingo, I could convince them in
five minutes that we wouldn't hurt them."

"If we could only signal," said Billy Fairfax, "that if they'd only come down to earth, we wouldn't go any nearer than they wanted. But the deuce of it is proving to them that we don't bite."

"It is probably that they have known only males of a more primitive type," Frank Merrill explained. "Possibly they are accustomed to marriage by capture."

"That would be a very lucky thing," Ralph explained in an aside to Honey. "Marriage by capture isn't such a foolish proposition, after all. Look at the Sabine women. I never heard tell that there was any kick coming from them. It all depends on the men."

"Oh, Lord, Ralph, marriage by capture isn't a sporting proposition," said Honey in a disgusted tone. "I'm not for it. A man doesn't get a run for his money. It's too much like shooting trapped game."

"Well, I will admit that there's more fun in the chase," Ralph answered.

"Oh, well, if the little darlings are not accustomed to chivalry from men," Pete Murphy was in the meantime saying, " that explains why they stand us off."

It was typical of Pete to refer to the flying-girls as " little darlings." The shortest among them was, of course, taller than he. But to Pete any woman was " little one," no matter what her stature, as any woman was " pure as the driven snow " until she proved the contrary. This impregnable simplicity explained much of the disaster of his married life.

" I am convinced," Frank Merrill said meditatively, " we must go about winning their confidence with the utmost care. One false step might be fatal. I know what your impatience is though— for I can hardly school myself to wait—that extraordinary phenomenon of the wings interests me so much. The great question in my mind is their position biologically and sociologically."

" The only thing that bothers me," Honey contributed solemnly, " is whether or not they're our social equals."

Even Frank Merrill laughed. " I mean, are

they birds," he went on still in a puzzled tone, "free creatures of the air, or women, bound creatures of the earth? And what should be our attitude toward them? Have we the right to capture them as ornithological specimens, or is it our duty to respect their liberty as independent human beings?"

"They're neither birds nor women," Pete Murphy burst out impetuously. "They're angels. Our duty is to fall down and worship them."

"They're women," said Billy Fairfax earnestly. "Our duty is to cherish and protect them."

"They're girls," Honey insisted jovially, "our duty is to josh and jolly them, to buy them taxi-cabs, theater-tickets, late suppers, candy, and flowers."

"They're females," said Ralph Addington contemptuously. "Our duty is to tame, subjugate, infatuate, and control them."

Frank Merrill listened to each with the look on his face, half perplexity, half irritation, which always came when the conversation took a humorous turn. " I am myself inclined to look upon them as an entirely new race of beings, requiring new laws," he said thoughtfully.

Although the quick appearance and the quick departure of the girls had upset the men temporarily, they went back to work at once. And as though inspired by their appearance, they worked like tigers. As before, they talked constantly of them, piling mountains of conjecture on molehills of fact. But now their talk was less of the wonder and the romance of the situation and more of the irritation of it. Ralph Addington's unease seemed to have infected them all. Frank Merrill had actually to coax them to keep at their duty of patrolling the beach. They were constantly studying the horizon for a glimpse of their strange visitors. Every morning they said, " I hope they'll come to-day "; every night, " Perhaps they'll come to-morrow." And always, " They won't put it over on us this time when we're not looking."

But in point of fact, the next visit of the flying-girls came when they least expected it—late in the evening.

It had been damp and dull all day. A high fog was gradually melting out of the air. Back of it a misty moon, more mature now, gleamed like a flask of honey in a golden veil. A few stars glimmered, placid, pale, and big. Suddenly between fog and earth—and they seemed to emerge from the mist like dreams from sleep—appeared the five dazzling girl-figures.

The fog had blurred the vividness of their plumage. The color no longer throbbed from wing-sockets to wing-tips; light no longer pulsated there. But great scintillating beads of fog-dew outlined the long curves of the wings, accentuated the long curves of the body. Hair, brows, lashes glittered as if threaded with diamonds. Their cheeks and lips actually glowed, luscious as ripe fruit.

"My God!" groaned Pete Murphy; "how beautiful and inaccessible! But women should be inaccessible," he ended with a sigh.

"Not so inaccessible as they were, though,"

Ralph Addington said. Again the appearance of the women had transformed him physically and mentally. He moved with the nervous activity of a man strung on wires. His brown eyes showed yellow gleams like a cat's. "They're flying lower and slower to-night."

It did seem as though the fog, light as it was, definitely impeded their wings. It gave to their movements a little languor that had a plaintive appealing quality. Perhaps they realized this themselves. In the midst of their aerial evolutions suddenly—and apparently without cause— they developed panic, turned seawards. Their audience, taken by surprise, burst into shouts of remonstrance, ran after them. The clamor and the motion seemed only to add to the girls' alarm. Their retreating speed was almost frenzied.

"What the—what's frightened them?" Honey Smith asked. Honey's brows had come together in an unaccustomed scowl. He bit his lips.

"Give it up," Billy Fairfax answered, and his tone boiled with exasperation. "I hope they haven't been frightened away for good."

"I think every time it's the last," exclaimed Pete Murphy, "but they keep coming back."

"Son," said Ralph Addington, and there was a perceptible element of patronage in his tone, "I'll tell you the exact order of events. It threw a scare into the girls to-night that they couldn't fly so well. But in an hour's time, they'll be sore because they didn't put up a good exhibition. Now, if I know anything at all about women— and maybe I flatter myself, but I think I know a lot—they'll be back the first thing to-morrow to prove to us that their bad flying was not our effect on them but the weather's."

Whether Ralph's theory was correct could not, of course, be ascertained. But in the matter of prophecy, he was absolutely vindicated. About half-way through the morning five black spots appeared in the west. They grew gradually to bewildering shapes and colors, for the girls came dressed in gowns woven of brilliant flowers. And the torrents of their beautiful hair floated loose. This time they held themselves grouped close; they kept themselves aloof, high. But again came

the sinuous interplay of flower-clad bodies, the
flashing evolution of rainbow wings, the dazzling
interweaving of snowy arms and legs. It held the
men breathless.

" They're like goldfish in a bowl," Billy Fairfax said. " I never saw such suppleness. You
wouldn't think they had a bone in their systems."

" I bet they're as strong as tigers, though,"
commented Addington. " I wouldn't want to
handle more than one of them at once."

" I think I could handle two," remarked Frank
Merrill. He said this, not boastfully, but as one
who states an interesting fact. And he spoke as
impersonally as though the girls were machines.

Ralph Addington studied Frank Merrill's gigantic copper-colored bulk enviously. " I guess
you could," he agreed.

" Fortunately," Frank went on, " it would be
impossible for such a situation to arise. Men
don't war on women."

" On the contrary," Ralph disagreed, " men always war on women, and women on men. Why,
Merrill," he added with his inevitable tone of

patronage, "aren't you wise to the fact that the war between the sexes is in reality more bitter and bloody than any war between the races?"

But Frank did not answer. He only stared.

"Did you notice," Pete Murphy asked, "what wonderful hair they had? Loose like that—they looked more than ever like Valkyries."

"Yes, I got that," Ralph answered. He smiled until all his white teeth showed. "And take it from me, that's a point gained. When a woman begins to let her hair down, she's interested."

"Well," said Honey Smith, "their game may be the same as every other woman's you've known, but it takes a damned long time to come down to cases. What I want to know is how many months more will have to pass before we speak when we pass by."

"That matter'll take care of itself," Ralph reassured him. "You leave it to natural selection."

"Well, it's a deuce of a slow process," Honey grumbled.

What hitherto had been devotion to their work grew almost to mania. It increased their interest that the little settlement of five cabins was fast taking shape. The men slept in beds now; for they had furnished their rooms. They had begun to decorate the walls. They re-opened the trunks and made another careful division of spoils. They were even experimenting with razors and quarreling amicably over their merits. At night, when their work was done, they actually changed their clothes.

"One week more of this," commented Honey Smith, "and we'll be serving meals in courses. I hope that our lady-friends will call sometime when we're dressed for dinner. I've tried several flossy effects in ties without results. But I expect to lay them out cold with these riding-boots."

Nevertheless many days passed and the flying-girls continued not to appear.

"I don't believe they're ever coming again," Pete Murphy said one day in a tone of despair.

"Oh, they'll come," Ralph Addington insisted. "They think themselves that they're not coming again, after having proved to us that they could

fly just as well as ever. But they'll appear sometime when we least expect it. There's something
pulling them over here that's stronger than anything they've ever come up against. They don't
know what it is, but we do—Mr. G. Bernard
Shaw's life-force. They haven't realized yet what
put the spoke in their wheel, but it will bring them
here in the end."

But days and days went by. The men worked
hard, in the main good-naturedly, but with occasional outbreaks of discontent and irritation.
"How about that proposition of the life-force?"
they asked Ralph Addington again and again.
"You wait!" was all he ever answered.

One day, Honey Smith, who had gone off for
a solitary walk, came running back to camp.
"What do you think?" he burst out when he got
within earshot. "I've seen one of them, the little
brunette, the one with the orange wings, the
'plain one.' She was flying on the other side of
the island all by her lonesome. She saw me first,
and as sure as I stand here, she called to me—a
regular bird-call. I whistled and she came flying

over in my direction. Blamed if she didn't keep right over my head for the whole trip."

"Low?" Ralph questioned eagerly.

"Yes," Honey answered succinctly, "but not low enough. I couldn't touch her, of course. If I stopped for a while and kept quiet as the dead, she'd come much closer. But the instant I made a move towards—bing!—she hit the welkin. But the way she rubbered. And, Lord, how easy scared. Once I waved my handkerchief—she nearly threw a fit. Strangest sensation I've ever had in my life to be walking calmly along like that with a girl beside me—*flying*. She isn't so plain when you get close—she does look like a Kanaka, though." He stopped and burst out laughing. "Funny thing! I kept calling her *Lulu*. After a while, she got it that that was her tag. She didn't exactly come closer when I said 'Lulu,' but she'd turn her head over her shoulder and look at me."

"Well, damn you and your *beaux yeux!*" said Ralph. There was a real chagrin behind the amusement in his voice.

"Did you notice the muscular development of

her back and shoulders?" Frank Merrill asked eagerly.

"No," said Honey regretfully, "I don't seem to remember anything but her face."

The next morning when they were working, Pete Murphy suddenly yelled in an excited voice, "Here comes one of them!"

Everybody turned. There, heading straight towards them, an unbelievable orange patch sailing through the blue sky, flew the "plain one."

"Lulu! Lulu! Here I am, Lulu," Honey called in his most coaxing tone and with his most radiant smile. Lulu did not descend, but, involuntarily it seemed, she turned her course a little nearer to Honey. She fluttered an instant over his head, then flew straight as an arrow eastward.

"She's a looker, all right, all right," Ralph Addington said, gazing as long as she was in sight. "I guess I'll trade my blonde for your brunette, Honey."

"I bet you won't," answered Honey. "I've got Lulu half-tamed. She'll be eating out of my hand in another week."

They found this incident exciting enough to justify them in laying off from work the rest of the afternoon. But they had to get accustomed to it in the week that followed. Thereafter, some time during the day, the cry would ring out, " Here's your girl, Honey! " And Honey, not even dropping his tools, would smile over his shoulder at the approaching Lulu.

As time went by, she ventured nearer and nearer, stayed longer and longer. Honey, calmly driving nails, addressed to her an endless, chaffing monologue. At first, it was apparent she was as much repelled by the tools as she was fascinated by Honey. For him to throw a nail to the ground was the signal for her to speed to the zenith. But gradually, in spite of the noise they made, she came to accept them as dumb, inanimate, harmless. And one day, when Honey, working on the roof, dropped a screw-driver, she flew down, picked it up, flew back, and placed it within reach of his hand. She would hover over him for hours, helping in many small ways. This only, however, when the other men were sufficiently far away and only when Honey's two hands were occupied. If any one of them— Honey and the rest—made the most casual of accidental moves in her direction, her flight was that of an arrow. But nobody could have been more careful than they not to frighten her.

They always stopped, however, to watch her approach and her departure. There was something irresistibly feminine about Lulu's flight. She herself seemed to appreciate this. If anybody looked at her, she exhibited her accomplishments with an eagerness that had a charming touch of naïveté. She dipped and dove endlessly. She dealt in little darts and rushes, bird-like in their speed and grace. She never flew high, but, on her level, her activity was marvelous.

" The supermanning little imp ! " Pete Murphy said again and again. " The vain little devil," Ralph Addington would add, chuckling.

" How the thunder did we ever start to call her the ' plain one '? " Honey was always asking in an injured tone.

Lulu was far from plain. She was, however,

one of those girls who start by being " ugly " or
" queer-looking," or downright " homely," and
end by becoming " interesting " or " picturesque "
or " fascinating," according to the divagations of
the individual vocabulary. She had the *beauté
troublante*. At first sight, you might have called
her gipsy, Indian, Kanaka, Chinese, Japanese,
Korean—any exotic type that you had not seen.
Which is to say that she had the look of the primitive woman and the foreign woman. Superficially, her beauty of irregularity was of all beauty
the most perturbing and provocative. Eyes, skin,
hair, she was all copper-browns and crimson-
bronzes, all the high gloss of satiny surfaces.
Every shape and contour was a variant from the
regular. Her eyes took a bewildering slant. Her
face showed a little piquant stress on the cheek-
bones. Her hair banded in a long, solid, club-
like braid. In repose she bore a look a little
sullen, a little heavy. When she smiled, it seemed
as if her whole face waked up; but it was only the
glitter of white teeth in the slit of her scarlet
mouth.

Lulu always dressed in browns and greens; leaves, mosses, grasses made a dim-colored, velvety fabric that contrasted richly with her coppery satin surfaces and her brilliant orange wings.

The excitement of this had hardly died down when Frank Merrill brought the tale of another adventure to camp. He had fallen into the habit of withdrawing late in the afternoon to one of the reefs, far enough away to read and to write quietly. One day, just as he had gone deep into his book, a shadow fell across it. Startled, he looked up. Directly over his head, pasted on the sky like a scarlet V, hovered the " dark one." After his first instant of surprise and a second interval of perplexity, he put his book down, settled himself back quietly, and watched. Conscious of his espionage apparently, she flew away, floated, flew back, floated, flew up, flew down, floated— always within a little distance. After half an hour of this aerial irresolution, she sailed off. She repeated her performance the next afternoon and the next, and the next, staying longer each time. By the end of the week she was spending whole afternoons there. She, too, became a regular visitor.

She never spoke. And she scarcely moved. She waved her great scarlet wings only fast enough to hold herself beyond Frank's reach. But from that distance she watched his movements, watched closely and unceasingly, watched with the interest of a child at a moving-picture show. Her surveillance of him was so intense it seemed impossible that she could see anything else. But if one of the other four men started to join them, she became a flash of scarlet lightning that tore the distance.

Frank, of course, found this interesting. Every day he made voluminous notes of his observations. Every night he embodied these notes in his monograph.

" What does she look like close to? " the others asked him again and again.

" Really, I've hardly had a chance to notice yet," was Frank's invariable answer. " She's a comely young person, I should say, and, as you can easily see, of the brunette coloring. I'm so much more interested in her flying than in her appearance that I've never really taken a good look at her. Unfortunately she flies less well than the others. I wish I could get a chance to study all of them— the ' quiet one ' in particular; she flies so much faster. On the other hand, this one seems able to hold herself motionless in the air longer than they."

" She's lazy," Honey Smith said decisively. " I got that right off. She looks like a Spanish woman and she is a good deal like one in her ways."

Honey was right; the " dark one " was lazy. Alone she always flew low, and at no time, even in company, did she dare great altitudes. She seemed to love to float, wings outspread and eyes half closed, on one of those tranquil air-plateaux that lie between drifting air-currents. She was an adept, apparently, at finding the little nodule of quiet space that forms the center of every wind-storm. Standing upright in it, flaming wings erect, she would whirl through space like an autumn leaf. Gradually, she became less suspicious of the other men. She often passed in their direction on the way to her afternoon vigil with Frank.

"She certainly is one peach of a female," said Ralph Addington. "I don't know but what she's prettier than my blonde. Too bad she's stuck on that stiff of a Merrill. I suppose he'd sit there every afternoon for a year and just look at her."

"I should think she came from Andalusia," Honey answered, watching the long, low sweep of her scarlet flight. "She's got to have a Spanish name. Say we call her Chiquita."

And Chiquita she became.

Chiquita was beautiful. Her beauty had a high-wayman quality of violence; it struck quick and full in the face. She was the darkest of all the girls, a raven black. As Lulu was all coppery shine and shimmer, all satiny gloss and gleam, so Chiquita was all dusk in the coloring, all velvet in the surfaces. Her great heavy-lidded eyes were dusk and velvet, with depth on depth of an un-meaning dreaminess. Her hair, brows, lashes were dusk and velvet; and there was no light in them. Her skin, a dusky cream on which velvety shade accented velvety shadow, was colorless except where her lips, cupped like a flower, offered a

splash of crimson. Yet, in spite of the violence
of her beauty, her expression held a tropical languor. Indeed, had not her flying compelled a
superficial vigor from her, she would have seemed
voluptuous.

Chiquita wore scarlet always, the exact scarlet
of her wings, a clinging mass of tropical bloom;
huge star-shaped or lily-like flowers whose brilliant lustre accentuated her dusky coloring.

They had no sooner accustomed themselves to
the incongruity of Frank Merrill's conquest of
this big, gorgeous creature than Pete Murphy developed what Honey called "a case." It was
scarcely a question of development; for with Pete
it had been the "thin one" from the beginning.
Following an inexplicable masculine vagary, he
christened her Clara—and Clara she ultimately became. Among themselves, the men employed
other names for her; with them she was not so
popular as with Pete. To Ralph she was "the
cat"; to Billy, "the poser"; to Honey, "Car-
rots."

Clara appeared first with Lulu. She did not

stay long on her initial visit. But afterwards she always accompanied her friend, always stayed as late as she.

"I'd pick those two for running-mates anywhere," Ralph said in private to Honey. "I wish I had a dollar bill for every time I've met up with that combination, one simple, devoted, self-sacrificing, the other selfish, calculating, catty."

Clara was not exactly beautiful, although she had many points of beauty. Her straight red hair clung to her head like a close-fitting helmet of copper. Her skin balanced delicately between a brown pallor and a golden sallowness. Her long, black lashes paled her gray eyes slightly; her snub nose made charming havoc of what, without it, would have been a conventional regularity of profile. She was really no more slender than the normal woman, but, compared with her mates, she seemed of elfin slimness; she was shapely in a supple, long-limbed way. There was something a little exotic about her. Her green and gold plumage gave her a touch of the fantastic and the bizarre. Prevailingly, she arrayed herself in flowers that ran all the shades from cream and lemon to yellow and orange. She was like a parrot among more uniformly feathered birds.

Clara never flew high. It was apparent, however, that if she made a tremendous effort, she could take any height. On the other hand, she flew more swiftly than either Lulu or Chiquita. She seemed to keep by preference to the middle altitudes. She hated wind and fog; she appeared only in calm and dry weather. Perhaps this was because the wind interfered with her histrionics, the fog with the wavy complications of her red hair. For she postured as she moved; whatever her hurry, she presented a picture, absolutely composed. And her hair was always intricately arranged, always decked with leaves and flowers.

" By jiminy, I'd make my everlasting fortune off you," Honey Smith once addressed her, as she flew over his head, " selling you to the moving-picture people."

Wings straight up, legs straight out, arms straight ahead, delicately slender feet, and strong-looking hands dropping like flowers, her only an-

swer to this remark was an enigmatic closing of
her thick-lashed lids, a twist into a pose even more
sensuously beautiful.

"Say, I'm tired waiting," Ralph Addington
growled one day, when the lovely trio flew over his
head in a group. "Why doesn't that blonde of
mine put in an appearance? Oh, Clara, Lulu,
Chiquita," he called, "won't you bring your
peachy friend the next time you call?"

It was a long time, however, before the "peachy
one" appeared. Then suddenly one day a great
jagged shadow enveloped them in its purple cool-
ness. The men looked up, startled. She must
have come upon them slowly and quietly, for she
was close. Her mischievous face smiled alluringly
down at them from the wide triangle of her blue
wings.

Followed an exhibition of flying which outdid
all the others.

Dropping like a star from the zenith and dropping so close and so swiftly that the men involuntarily scattered to give her landing-room, she
caught herself up within two feet of their heads

and bounded straight up to the zenith again. Up she went, and up and up until she was only a blue shimmer; and up and up and up until she was only a dark dot. Then, without warning, again she dropped, gradually this time, head-foremost like a diver, down and down and down until her body was perfectly outlined, down and down and down until she floated just above their heads.

Coming thus slowly upon them, she gave, for the first time, a close view of her wonderful blondeness. It was a sheer golden blondeness, not a hint of tow, or flaxen, or yellow; not a touch of silver, or honey, or auburn. It was half her charm that the extraordinary strength and vigor of her contours contrasted with the delicacy and dewiness of her coloring, that from one aspect, she seemed as frail as a flower, from another as hard as a crystal. She had, at the same time, the untouched, unstained beauty of the virgin girl, and the hard, muscular strength of the virgin boy. Her skin, white as a lily-petal and as thick and smooth, had been deepened by a single drop of amber to cream. Her eyes, of which the sculpturesque lids drooped a little, flashed a blue as limpid as the sky. Teeth, set as close as seed-pearls, gleamed between lips which were the pink of the faded rose. The sunlight turned her golden hair to spun glass, melted it to light itself. The shadow thickened it to fluid, hardened it to massy gold again. The details of her face came out only as the result of determined study. Her chief beauty—and it amounted to witchery, to enchantment—lay in a constant and a constantly subtle change of expression.

During this exhibition the men stood frozen in the exact attitudes in which she found them. Ralph Addington alone remained master of himself. He stood quiet, every nerve tense, every muscle alert, the expression on his face that of a cat watching a bird. At her second dip downward, he suddenly jumped into the air, jumped so high that his clutching fingers grazed her finger-tips.

That frightened her.

Her upward flight was of a terrific speed—she leaped into the sky. But once beyond the danger-line her composure came back. She dropped on them a coil of laughter, clear as running water, contemptuous, mischievous. Still laughing, she sank again, almost as near. Her mirth brought her lids close together. Her eyes, sparkling between thick files of golden lash, had almost a cruel sweetness.

She immediately flew away, departing over the water. Ralph cursed himself for the rest of the day. She returned before the week was out, however, and, after that, she continued to visit them at intervals of a few days. The sudden note of blue, even in the distance it seemed to connote coquetry, was the signal for all the men to stop work. They could not think clearly or consecutively when she was about. She was one of those women whose presence creates disturbance, perturbation, unrest. The very sunshine seemed alive, the very air seemed vibrant with her. Even when she flew high, her shadow came between them and their work.

"She sure qualifies when it comes to fancy flying," said Honey Smith. "She's in a class all by herself.

Her flying was daring, eccentric, temperamental, the apotheosis of brilliancy—genius. The sudden dart up, the terrifying drop down seemed her main accomplishment. The wonder of it was that the men could never tell where she would land. Did it seem that she was aiming near, a sudden swoop would bring her to rest on a far-away spot. Was it certain that she was making for a distant tree-top, an unexpected drop would land her a few feet from their group. She was the only one of the flying-girls who touched the earth. And she always led up to this feat as to the climax of what Honey called her " act." She would drop to the very ground, pose there, wavering like an enormous butterfly, her great wings opening and shutting. Sometimes, tempted by her actual nearness and fooled by her apparent weakness, the five men would make a rush in her direction. She would stand waiting and drooping until they were almost on her. Then in a flash came the tremendous whirr of her start, the violent beat of her whipping progress—she had become a blue speck.

She wore always what seemed to be gossamer,

rose-color in one light, sky-color in another; a flexible film that one moment defined the long slim lines of her body and the next concealed them completely. Near, it could be seen that this drapery was woven of tiny buds, pink and blue; afar she seemed to float in a shimmering opalescent mist.

She teased them all, but it was evident from the beginning that she had picked Ralph to tease most. After a long while, the others learned to ignore, or to pretend to ignore, her tantalizing overtures. But Ralph could look at nothing else while she was about. She loved to lead him in a long, wild-goose chase across the island, dipping almost within reach one moment, losing herself at the zenith in another, alighting here and there with a will-o'-the-wisp capriciousness. Sometimes Ralph would return in such an exhausted condition that he dropped to sleep while he ate. At such times his mood was far from agreeable. His companions soon learned not to address him after these expeditions.

One afternoon, exercising heroic resolution, Ralph allowed Peachy to fly, apparently unnoticed,

over his head, let her make an unaccompanied
way half across the island. But when she had
passed out of earshot he watched her carefully.

"Say, Honey," he said after half an hour's
fidgeting, "Peachy's settled down somewhere on
the island. I should say on the near shore of the
lake. I don't know that anything's happened—
probably nothing. But I hope to God," he added
savagely, "she's broken a wing. Come on and
find out what she's up to, will you?"

"Sure!" Honey agreed cheerfully. "All's fair
in love and war. And this seems to be *both* love
and war."

They walked slowly, and without talking, across
the beach. When they reached the trail they
dropped on all fours and pulled themselves noiselessly along. The slightest sound, the snapping
of a twig, the flutter of a bird, brought them to
quiet. An hour, they searched profitlessly.

Then suddenly they got sound of her, the
languid slap of great wings opening and shutting.
She had not gone to the lake. Instead, she had
chosen for her resting-place one of the tiny pools

which, like pendants of a necklace, partially encircled the main body. She was sitting on a flat
stone that projected into the water. Her
drooped blue wings, glittering with moisture, had
finally come to rest; they trailed behind her over
the gray boulder and into a mass of vivid green
water-grasses. One bare shoulder had broken
through her rose-and-blue drapery. The odor of
flowers came from her. Her hair, a braid over
each breast, oozed like ropes of melted gold to her
knees. A hand held each of these braids. She was
evidently preoccupied. Her eyelids were down.
Absently she dabbled her white feet in the water.
The noise of her splashing covered their approach.
The two men signaled their plans, separated.

Five minutes went by, and ten and fifteen and
twenty. Peachy still sat silent, moveless, medi-
tative. Not once did she lift her eyelids.

Then Addington leaped like a cat from the
bushes at her right. Simultaneously Honey
pounced in her direction from the left.

But—whir-r-r-r—it was like the beating of a tremendous drum. Straight across the pond she went,

her toes shirring the water, and up and up and up—then off. And all the time she laughed, a delicious, rippling laughter which seemed to climb every scale that could carry coquetry.

The two men stood impotently watching her for a moment. Then Honey broke into roars of delight. "Oh, you kid!" he called appreciatively to her. "She had her nerve with her to sit still all the time, knowing that we were creeping up on her, didn't she?" He turned to Ralph.

But Ralph did not answer, did not hear. His face was black with rage. He shook his fist in Peachy's direction.

Of the flying-girls, there remained now only one who held herself aloof, the "quiet one." It was many weeks before she visited the island. Then she came often, though always alone. There was something in her attitude that marked her off from the others.

"She doesn't come because she wants to," Billy Fairfax explained. "She comes because she's lonely."

The "quiet one" habitually flew high and kept

high, so high indeed that, after the first excitement of her tardy appearance, none but Billy gave
her more than passing attention. Up to that time
Billy had been a hard, a steady worker. But now
he seemed unable to concentrate on anything. It
was doubtless an extra exasperation that the
" quiet one " puzzled him. Her flying seemed
to be more than a haphazard way of passing
the time. It seemed to have a meaning; it
was almost as if she were trying to accomplish
something by it; and ever she perfected the figure
that her flight drew on the sky. If she soared
and dropped, she dropped and soared. If she
curved and floated, she floated and curved. If she
dipped and leaped, she leaped and dipped. All
this he could see. But there were scores of minor
evolutions that appeared to him only as confused
motion.

One thing he caught immediately. Those lonely
gyrations were not the exercise of the elusive coquetry which distinguished Peachy. It was more
that the " quiet one " was pushed on by some intel-
lectual or artistic impulse, that she expressed by

the symbols of her complicated flight some theory, some philosophy of life, that she traced out some artless design, some primary pattern of beauty.

Julia always seemed to shine; she wore garments of gleamy-petalled, white flowers, silvery seaweeds, pellucid marsh-grasses, vines, golden or purple, that covered her with a delicate lustre. Her wings were different from the others; theirs flashed color, but hers gave light; and that light seemed to have run down on her flesh.

"What the thunder is she trying to do up there?" Ralph asked one day, stopping at Billy's side. Ralph's question was not in reality begotten so much of curiosity as of irritation. From the beginning the "quiet one" had interested him least of any of the flying-girls as, from the beginning, Peachy had interested him most.

"I don't know, of course." Billy spoke with reluctance. It was evident that he did not enjoy discussing the "quiet one" with Ralph. "At first my theory was that flying was to her what dancing is to most girls. But, somehow, it seems to go deeper than that—as if it were art, or even creation. Anyway, there's a kind of bi-lateral symmetry about everything she does."

Billy fell into the habit, each afternoon, of strolling away from the rest, out of sound of their chaff. On the grassy top of one of the reefs, he found a spot where he could lie comfortably and watch the " quiet one." He used to spin long daydreams there. She looked so remote far up in the boiling blue, and so strange, that he had an inexplicable sensation of reverence.

Now it was as though, in watching that aerial weaving and interweaving, he were assisting at a religious rite. He liked it best when the white day-moon was afloat. If he half-shut his eyes, it seemed to him that she and the moon made twin crescents of foaming silver, twin bubbles of white fire, twin films of fairy gossamer, twin vials that held the very essence of poetry. Somehow he had always connected her with the moon. Indeed, in her whiteness, her coldness, her aloofness, she seemed the very sublimation of virginity. His first secret names for her were Diana and Cynthia. But there was another quality in her that those

names did not include—intellectuality. His favorite heroes were Julius Cæsar and Edwin Booth
—a quaint pair, taken in combination. In the long
imaginary conversations which he held with her
he addressed her as Julia or Edwina.

Days and days went by and he could discover
no sign that she had noticed him. It was typical
of the " damned gentleman " side of Billy that he
did not try to attract her attention. Indeed, his
efforts were ever to efface himself.

One afternoon, after a long vigil in which, un-
accountably, Julia had not appeared, he started
to return to camp. It was a late twilight and a
black, velvety one. The trees against a darkening
curtain of sky had turned to bunches of tangled
shadow, the reefs and rocks against the papery
white of the sand to smutches and blobs of soot.
Suddenly—and his heart pounded at the sound—
the air began to vibrate and thrill.

He stopped short. He waited. His breath
came fast; the vibration and thrill were coming
closer.

He crystallized where he stood. It scarcely seemed that he breathed. And then——

Something white and nebulous came floating out of the dusk towards him. It became a silver cloud, a white sculptured spirit of the air. It became an angel, a fairy, a woman—Julia. She flew not far off, level with his eyes and, as she approached, she slowed her stately flight. Billy made no movement. He only stood and waited and watched. But perhaps never before in his life had his eyes become so transparently the windows of his soul. Quite as intently, Julia's eyes, big, gray, and dark-lashed, considered him. It seemed to Billy that he had never seen in any face so virginally young such a tragic seriousness, nor in any eyes, superficially so calm, such a troubled wonder.

He did not stir until she had drifted out of ear-shot, had become again a nebulous silver cloud drifting into the dusk, had merged with that dusk.

" What makes your eyes shine so ? " said Honey, examining him keenly when he reached camp.

It was the first time Billy had known Julia to fly low. But he discovered gradually that only in the sunlight did she haunt the zenith. At twilight she always kept close to the earth. Billy took to haunting the reefs at dusk.

Again and again, the same thing happened.

Suddenly—and it was as if successive waves of electricity charged through his body—the quiet air began to purr and vibrate and drum. Out of the star-shot dusk emerged the speeding whiteness of Julia. Always, as she approached, she slowed her flight. Always as she passed, her sorrowing gray eyes would seek his burning blue ones. Billy could bring himself to speak of this strange experience to nobody, not even to Honey. For there was in it something untellable, unsharable, the wonder of the vision and the dream, the unreality of the apparition.

The excitement of these happenings kept the men entertained, but it also kept them keyed up to high tension. For a while they did not notice this themselves. But when they attempted to go back to their interrupted work, they found it hard to concentrate upon it. Frank Merrill had given up trying to make them patrol the beach. Unaided, day and night he attended to their signals.

"Well," said Honey Smith one day and, for the first time, there was a peevish note in his voice, "that 'natural selection' theory of yours, Ralph, seems to have worked out to some extent—but not enough. We seem to be comfortably divided, all ten of us, into happy couples, but hanged if I'm strong for this long-distance acquaintance."

"You're right there," Ralph Addington admitted; "we don't seem to be getting any forwarder."

"It's all very pretty and romantic to have these girls flying about," Honey continued in a grumbling tone, "but it's too much like flirting with a canary-bird. Damn it all, I want to talk with them."

Ralph made a hopeless gesture. "It *is* a deadlock, I admit. I'm at my wits' end."

Perhaps Honey expressed what the others felt. At any rate, a sudden irascibility broke out among them. They were good-natured enough while the girls were about, but over their work and during their leisure, they developed what Honey described

as " every kind of blue-bean, sourball, katzenjam-
mer *and* grouch." They fought heroically against
it—and their method of fighting took various
forms, according to the nature of the four men.
Frank Merrill lost himself in his books. Pete
Murphy began the score of an opera vaguely
heroic in theme; he wrote every spare moment.
Billy Fairfax worked so hard that he grew thin.
Honey Smith went off on long, solitary walks.
Ralph Addington, as usual, showed an exasperat-
ing tendency towards contradiction, an unvarying
contentiousness.

And then, without warning, all the girls ceased
to come to the island. Three days went by, five,
a week, ten days. One morning they all passed
over the island, one by one, an hour or two between
flights; but they flew high and fast, and they did
not stop.

Ralph Addington had become more and more
irascible. That day the others maintained peace
only by ignoring him.

" By the gods! " he snarled at night as they all
sat dull and dumb about the fire. " Something's

got to happen to change our way of living or murder'll break out in this community. And we'd better begin pretty quick to do something about it. What I'd like to know is," and he slapped his hand smartly against a flat rock, " coming down to cases—as we must sooner or later—what is our *right* in regard to these women."

III

" I DON'T exactly like your use of the word *right*, Ralph," said Billy. " You mean *duty*, don't you? "

" And he'd better change that to *privilege*," put in Pete Murphy, scowling.

" Shut up, you mick," Honey interposed, flicking Pete on the ear with a pebble. " What do you know about machinery? "

Pete grinned and subsided for a moment. Honey could always placate him by calling him a " mick."

" No," Ralph went on obstinately, addressing himself this time to Billy, " I mean *right*. Of course, I mean right," he went on with one of his gusty bursts of irritation. " For God's sake, don't be so high-brow and altruistic."

" How about it, Frank? " Billy said, turning to Merrill.

"Well," said Frank slowly, "I don't exactly know how to answer that question. I don't know what you mean by the word—*right*. I take it that you mean what our right would be if these flying-maidens permitted themselves to become our friends. I would say, that, in such a case, you would have the only right that any man ever has, as far as women are concerned—the right to woo. If he wins, all well and good. If he loses, he must abide by the consequences."

"You're on, Frank," said Billy Fairfax. "You've said the last word."

"In normal condition, I'd agree with you," Ralph said. "But in these conditions I disagree utterly."

"How?" Frank asked. "Why?" He turned to Ralph with the instinctive equability that he always presented to an opponent in argument.

"Well, in the first place, we find ourselves in a situation unparalleled in the world's history." Ralph had the air of one who is saying aloud for the first time what he has said to himself many times. At any rate, he proceeded with an unusual fluency and glibness. " Circumstances alter cases. We can't handle this situation by any of the standards we have formerly known. In fact, we've got to throw all our former standards overboard. There are five of these girls. There are five of us. *Voilà!* Following the laws of nature we have selected each of us the mates we prefer. Or, following the law that Bernard Shaw discovered, the ladies have selected, each of them, the mates that they prefer. They are now turning themselves inside out to prove to us that we selected them. *Voilà!* The rest is obvious. If they come to terms, all right! If they don't——" He paused. " I repeat that we are placed in a situation new in the history of the world. I repeat the bromidion—circumstances alter cases. We may have to stay on this island as long as we live. I am perfectly willing to confess that just now I'd rather not be rescued. But it's over four months that we've been here. We must think of the future. The future justifies anything. If these girls don't come to terms, they must be made to come to terms. You'll find I'm right."

"Right!" exclaimed Billy hotly. "What are you talking about? Those are the principles of an Apache or a Hottentot."

" Or a cave-man," Pete added.

"Well, what are we under our skins but Hottentots and Apaches and cave-men?" said Ralph. "Now, I leave it to you. Look facts in the face. Use your common sense. Count out civilization and all its artificial rules. Think of our situation on this island, if we don't capture these women soon. We can't tell when they'll stop coming. We don't know what the conditions of their life may be. The caprice may strike them to-morrow to cut us out for good. Maybe their men will discover it—and prevent them from coming. A lot of things may happen to keep them away. What's to become of us in that case? We'll go mad, five men alone here. It isn't as though we could tame them by any gentle methods. You can't catch eagles by putting salt on their tails. In the first place, we can't get close enough to them, because of their accursed wings, to prove that we wouldn't harm them. They've sent us a challenge—it's a magnificent one. They've thrown down the gage. And how have we responded? I bet they think we're a precious lot of molly-coddles! I bet they're laughing in their sleeves all the time. I'd hate to hear what they say about us. But the point I'm trying to make is not that. It's this: we can't afford to lose them. This place is a prison now. It will be worse than that if this keeps up—it'll be a madhouse."

"Do you mean to tell me that you're advocating marriage by capture?" Billy asked in an incredulous voice.

"I mean to tell you I'm arguing *capture*," Ralph said with emphasis. "After that, you can trust the marriage question to take care of itself."

Argument broke out hydra-headed. They wrangled the whole evening. Theory at first guided them. In the beginning, names like Plato, Nietzsche, Schopenhauer preceded quotation; then, came Shaw, Havelock-Ellis, Kraft-Ebing, Weininger. Sleep deadened their discussion temporarily but it burst out at intervals all the next day. In fact, it seemed to possess eternal vitality, eternal fascination. Leaving theory, they went for parallels of their strange situation, to history, to the Scriptures, to fiction, to drama, to poetry.

Honey ended every discussion with a philosophic, " Aside from the question of brutality, this marriage by capture isn't a sporting proposition. It's like jacking deer. I'm not for it. And, O Lord, what's the use of chewing the rag so much about it? Wait a while. We'll get them yet, I betchu!"

All of Honey's sex-pride flared in this buoyant assurance. It had apparently not yet occurred to him that he would not conquer Lulu in the end and conquer her by merely submitting to her wooing of him.

And in the meantime, the voiceless tête-à-tête-ing of the five couples continued.

" Say, Ralph," Honey said one day in a calm interval, " it's just occurred to me that we haven't seen those girls flying in a bunch for quite some time. Don't suppose they've quarrelled, do you?"

Everybody stopped work to stare at him. " I bet that's the answer," Ralph exclaimed. His voice held the note of one for whom a private mystification has at last broken.

"But what do you suppose they've quarrelled about?" Pete Murphy asked.

"Me," Honey said promptly.

Ralph laughed absent-mindedly. "It's a hundred to one shot that they're quarrelling about us, though," he said. For some mysterious reason this theory raised his spirits perceptibly.

"But—to get down to brass tacks," Pete asked in a puzzled tone, "what have we done to make them quarrel?"

"Oh, we've done nothing," Ralph answered with one of his lordly assumptions of a special knowledge. "It's just the disorganization that always falls on women when men appear on their horizon. They're absolutely without sex-loyalty, you know. They seem to have principle enough in regard to some things, a few things. But the moment a man appears, it's all off. West of Suez, they'll lie and steal; east of Suez, they'll betray and murder as easy as breathe."

"Cut that out, Addington," Pete Murphy commanded in a dangerous voice. "I won't stand for that kind of talk."

Ralph glared. "Won't stand for it?" he repeated. "I'd like to know how the hell you're going to help yourself?"

"I'll find, a way, and pretty damned quick," Pete retorted.

It was the closest approach to a quarrel that had yet occurred. The other three men hastily threw themselves into the breach. "Shut up, you mick," Honey called to Pete. "Remember you came over in the steerage."

Pete grinned and subsided.

"As sure as shooting," Honey said, "those girls have quarrelled. I bet we never see them again."

It was a long time before they saw any of them; but, curiously enough, the next time the flying-girls visited the island they came in a group.

It had been sultry, the first of a long series of sticky, muggy days. What threatened to be a thunderstorm and then, as Honey said, failed to "make good," came up in the afternoon. Just as the sky was at its blackest, Honey called, " Hurroo! Here they come!"

The effect of the approach of the flying-maidens was so strange as to make them unfamiliar. There was no sun to pour a liquid iridescence through their wings. All the high lights of their plumage had dulled. Painted in flat primary colors, they looked like paper dolls pasted on the inky thundercloud. As usual, when they came in a group, they wove in and out in a limited spherical area, achieving extraordinary effects in close wheeling.

As the girls made for the island, a new impulse seized Honey. He ran down the beach, dashed into the water, swam out to meet them.

"Come back, you fool!" Frank yelled. "There may be sharks in that water.

But Honey only laughed. He was a magnificent swimmer. He seemed determined to give, in an alien element, an exhibition which would equal that of the flying-girls. The effect on them was immediate; they broke ranks and floated, watching every move.

To hold their interest, Honey nearly turned himself inside out.

At first he tore the water white with the vigor of his trudgeon-stroke. Then turning from left to right, he employed the side-stroke. From that, he went to the breast-stroke. Last of all, he floated, dove, swam under water so long that the girls began uneasily to fly back and forth, to twitter with alarm.

Finally he emerged and floated again.

" He swims like a motor-boat! " said Ralph admiringly.

Suddenly Lulu fluttered away from her companions, dropped so low that she could have touched Honey with her hand, and flew protectingly above him.

The men on the beach watched these proceedings with a gradual diminution of their alarm, with the admiration that Honey in the water always excited, with the amusement that Lulu's fearless display of infatuation always developed.

" Oh, my God! " Frank called suddenly. " There's a shark! "

Simultaneously, the others saw what he saw—a sinister black triangle swiftly shearing the water. They ran, yelling, down to the water's edge and stood there trying to shout a warning over the noise of the surf.

Honey did not get it at once. He was still floating, his smiling, up-turned face looking into Lulu's smiling, down-turned one. Then, rolling over, he apparently caught a glimpse of the black fin bearing so steadily on him. He made immediately for the shore but he had swum far and fast.

Lulu was slower even than he in realizing the situation. For a moment, obviously piqued at his action, she dropped and hung in the rear. Perhaps her mates signaled to her, perhaps her intuition flashed the warning. Suddenly she looked back. The scream which she emitted was as shrill with terror as any wingless woman's. Swooping down like an eagle, she seized Honey under the shoulders, lifted him out of the water. His weight crippled her. For though the first impulse of her terror carried her high, she sank at once until Honey hung just above the water.

And continuously she screamed.

The other girls realized her plight in an instant. They dropped like stones to her side, eased her partially of Honey's weight. Julia alone did not touch him. She floated above, calling directions. The group of girls arose gradually, flew swiftly over the water toward the beach. The men ran to meet them.

"Don't go any further," Billy commanded in a peremptory voice unusual with him. "They'll not put him down if we come too near."

The men hesitated, stopped.

Immediately the girls deposited Honey on the sand.

"Did you notice the cleverness of that break-away?" said Pete. "He couldn't have got a clinch in anywhere."

But to do Honey justice, he attempted nothing of the sort. He lay flat and still until his rescuers were at a safe height. Then he sat up and smiled radiantly at them. "Ladies, I thank you," he said.

"And I'll see that you get a Carnegie medal if it takes the rest of my life. I guess," he remarked unabashed, as his companions joined him, "it will be fresh-water swimming for your little friend hereafter."

Nobody spoke for a while. His companions were still white and Billy Fairfax even shook.

"You looked like an engraving that used to hang over my bed when I was a child," said Ralph, with an attempt at humor that had, coming from him, a touching quality, "a bunch of angels lugging a dead man to heaven. You'd have been a ringer for it if you'd had a shave."

"Well, the next time the girls come, I'm going to swim out among the pretty sharks," said Pete, obviously trying to echo Ralph's light note. "By Jove, hear them chatter up there. They're talking all at once and at the top of their lungs just like your sisters and your cousins and your aunts."

"They're as pale as death, too," observed Billy. "Look at that!"

The flying-maidens had come together in a compact circular group, hands over each other's shoulders, wings faintly fluttering. Perceptibly they clung to each other for support. Their faces had turned chalky; their heads drooped. Intertwined thus, they drifted out of sight.

"Lord, they are beautiful, close-to!" Honey said. "You never saw such complexions! Or such eyes and teeth! And—and—by George, such an effect of purity and stainlessness. I feel like a—and yet, by——" He fell into an abstraction so deep that it was as though he had forgotten his companions.

For several days, the girls did not appear on Angel Island. All that time, the capture argument lay in abeyance. Even Ralph, who had introduced the project, seemed touched by the gallantry of Honey's rescue. Honey, himself, was strangely subdued; his eternal monologue had dried up; he seemed preoccupied. Nevertheless, it was he, who, one night, reopened the discussion with a defiant flat: "Well, boys, I might as well tell you, I've swung over to Ralph's side. I'm for the capture of those girls, and capture as soon as we can make it."

"Well, I'll be——" said Billy. "After they saved your life! Honey, I guess I don't know you any more."

"What's changed you?" Pete asked in amazement.

"Can't tell you why—don't know myself why—when you get the answer tell me. Only in the ten minutes that those girls packed me through the air, I did some quick thinking. I can't explain to you why we've got the right to capture them. But we have. That's all there is to it."

War broke out with a new animosity; for they had, of course, now definitely divided into sides. Their conversation always turned into argument now, no matter how peaceably and innocently it began.

The girls had begun to visit the island again, singly now, singly always. Discussion died down temporarily and the wordless tête-à-têteing began again. Lulu hovered ever at Honey's shoulder. Clara postured always within Pete's vision. Chiquita took up her eternal vigil on Frank's reef. Peachy discovered new wonders of what Honey

called " trick flying." Julia became a fixed white
star in their blue noon sky.

A day or two or three of this long-distance wooing, and argument exploded more vehemently than
ever. Honey and Ralph still maintained that, as
the ruling sex of a man-managed world, they had
the right of discovery to these women. Frank still
maintained that, as a supra-human race, the flying-
girls were subject to supra-human laws. Billy
and Pete still maintained that, as the development
not only of the race but of the individual de-
pended on the treatment of the female by the male,
the capture of these independent beings at this
stage of civilization would be a return to bar-
barism.

After one night of wrangling, they came to the
agreement that no one of them would take steps
towards capture until all five had consented to it.
They drew up a paper to this effect and signed it.

Their cabins were nearly completed now.
Boundless leisure threatened to open before them.
More and more in the time which they were alone
they fell into the habits which their individual

tastes developed.   Frank still worked on his library.   He had transferred the desk and the book-
cases to the interior of his hut.   He spent all his
spare time there arranging, classifying, and cata-
loguing his books.   Billy fell into an orgy of furni-
ture-making and repairing.   Addington began, unaided, to build a huge cabin, bigger than the
others, and separated a little distance from them.
Nobody asked him what it was for.   Honey took
long solitary walks into the interior of the island.
He returned with great bunches of uprooted flowers which he planted against the cabin-walls.   Pete
dragged out from an unexplored trunk a box of
water-colors, a block of paper.   Now, when he
was not working on a symphonic poem, he was
coping with the wonders of the semi-tropical coloring.   His companions rallied and harried him,
especially about the poem; but he could always
silence them with a threat to read it aloud.   All
the Celt in him had come to the surface.
They heard him chanting his numbers in the
depths of the forest; sometimes he intoned them,
swinging on the branch of a high tree.   He even

wandered over the reefs, reciting them to the waves.

One day, late in the afternoon, Billy lay on his favorite spot on the southern reef, dreaming. High up in the air, Julia flashed and gyrated, revolved and spun. It seemed to Billy that he had never seen her go so high. She looked like a silver feather. But as he looked, she went higher and higher, so high that she disappeared vertically.

A strange sense of loneliness fell on Billy. This was the first time since she had begun to come regularly to the island that she had cut their tryst short. He waited. She did not appear. A minute went by. Another and another and another. His sense of loneliness deepened to uneasiness. Still there was no sign of Julia. Uneasiness became alarm. Ah, there she was at last—a speck, a dot, a spot, a splotch. How she was flying! How——

Like a bullet the conviction struck him.

She was falling!

Memories of certain biplanic explorations surged into his mind. "She's frozen," he thought to himself. "She can't move her wings!" Terror paralyzed him; horror bound him. He stood still—numb, dumb, helpless.

Down she came like an arrow. Her wings kept straight above her head, moveless, still. He could see her breast and shoulders heave and twist, and contort in a fury of effort. Underneath her were the trees. He had a sudden, lightning-swift vision of a falling aviator that he had once seen. The horror of what was coming turned his blood to ice. But he could not move; nor could he close his eyes.

"Oh, God! Oh, God! Oh, God!" he groaned. And, finally, "Oh, thank God!"

Julia's wings were moving. But apparently she still had little control of them. They flapped frantically a half-minute; but they had arrested her fall; they held her up. They continued to support her, although she beat about in jagged circles. Alternately floating and fluttering, she caught on an air-current, hurled herself on it, floated; then, as though she were sliding through some gigantic pillar of quiet air, sank earthwards. She seized the topmost bough of one of the high trees, threw her arms across it and hung limp. She panted; it seemed as if her breasts must burst. Her eyes closed; but the tears streamed from under her eyelids.

Billy ran close. He made no attempt to climb the tree to which she clung, so weakly accessible. But he called up to her broken words of assurance, broken phrases of comfort that ended in a wild harangue of love and entreaty.

After a while her breath came back. She pulled herself up on the bough and sat huddled there, her eyelids down, her silvery fans drooping, the great mass of her honey-colored hair drifting over the green branches, her drapery of white lilies, slashed and hanging in tatters, the tears still streaming. Except for its ghastly whiteness, her face showed no change of expression. She did not sob or moan, she did not even speak; she sat relaxed. The tears stopped flowing gradually. Her eyelids lifted. Her eyes, stark and dark in her white face, gazed straight down into Billy's eyes.

And then Billy *knew*.

He stood moveless staring up at her; never, perhaps, had human eyes asked so definite a question or begged so definite a boon.

She sat moveless, staring straight down at him. But her eyes continued to withhold all answer, all reassurance.

After a while, she stirred and the spell broke. She opened and shut her wings half a dozen times before she ventured to leave her perch. But once in the air, all her strength, physical and mental, seemed to come back. She shook the hair out of her eyes. She pulled her drapery together. For a moment, she lingered near, floating, almost moveless, white, shining, carved, chiseled: like a marvelous piece of aerial sculpture. Then a flush of a delicate dawn-pink came into her white face. She caught the great tumbled mass of hair in both hands, tied it about her head. Swift as a flash of lightning, she turned, wheeled, soared, dipped. And for the first time, Billy heard her laugh. Her laughter was like a child's —gleeful. But each musical ripple thrust like a knife into his heart.

He watched her cleave the distance, watched her

disappear. Then, suddenly, a curious weakness
came over him. His head swam and he could not
see distinctly. Every bone in his body seemed to
repudiate its function; his flexed muscles slid him
gently to the earth. Time passed. After a while
consciousness came back. His dizziness ceased.
But he lay for a long while, face downward, his
forehead against the cool moss. Again and again
that awful picture came, the long, white, girl-
shape shooting earthwards, the ghastly, tortured
face, the frenzied, heaving shoulders. It was to
come again many times in the next week, that picture, and for years to make recurrent horror in
his sleep.

He returned to the camp white, wrung, and
weak. Apparently his companions had been
busy at their various occupations. Nobody had seen
Julia's fall; at least nobody mentioned it. After
dinner, when the nightly argument broke into its
first round, he was silent for a while. Then, " Oh,
I might as well tell you, Frank, and you, Pete," he
said abruptly, " that I've gone over to the other
side. I'm for capture, friendship by capture, mar-

riage by capture—whatever you choose to call it—but capture."

The other four stared at him. "What's happened to you and Ju——" Honey began. But he stopped, flushing.

Billy paid no attention to the bitten-off end of Honey's question. "Nothing's happened to me," he lied simply and directly. "I don't know why I've changed, but I have. I think this is a case where the end justifies the means. Women don't know what's best for them. We do. Unguided, they take the awful risks of their awful ignorance. Moreover, they are the conservative sex. They have no conscious initiative. These flying-women, for instance, have plenty of physical courage but no mental or moral courage. They hold the whip-hand, of course, now. Anything might happen to them. This situation will prolong itself indefinitely unless—unless we beat their cunning by our strategy." He paused. "I don't think they're competent to take care of themselves. I think it's our duty to take care of them. I think the sooner——" He paused again. "At the same time, I'm prepared to keep to our agreement. I won't take a step in this matter until we've all come round to it."

" If it wasn't for their wings," Honey said.

Billy shuddered violently. " If it wasn't for their wings," he agreed.

Frank bore Billy's defection in the spirit of classic calm with which he accepted everything. But Pete could not seem to reconcile himself to it. He was constantly trying to draw Billy into debate.

" I won't argue the matter, Pete," Billy said again and again. " I can't argue it. I don't pretend even to myself that I'm reasonable or logical, or just or ethical. It's only a feeling or an instinct. But it's too strong for me. I can't fight it. It's as if I'd taken a journey drugged and blindfolded. I don't know how I got on this side—but I'm here."

The effect of this was to weaken a little the friendship that had grown between Billy and Pete. Also Honey pulled a little way from Ralph and slipped nearer to his old place in Billy's regard.

But now there were three warring elements in camp. Honey, Ralph, and Billy hobnobbed constantly. Frank more than ever devoted himself to his reading. Pete kept away from them all, writing furiously most of the day.

"We're going to have a harder time with him than with Frank," Billy remarked once.

"I guess we can leave that matter to take care of itself," Ralph said with one of his irritating superior smiles. "How about it, Honey?"

"Surest thing you know," Honey answered reassuringly. "All you've got to do is wait—believe muh!"

"It does seem as if we'd waited pretty long," Honey himself fumed two weeks later, "I say we three get together and repudiate that agreement."

"That would be dishonorable," Billy said, "and foolish. You can see for yourself that we cannot stir a step in this matter without co-operation. As opponents, Pete and Frank could warn the girls off faster than we could lure them on."

"That's right, too," agreed Honey. "But I'm damned tired of this," he added drearily.

"Not more tired than we are," said Billy.

An incident that varied the monotony of the deadlock occurred the next day. Pete Murphy packed up food and writing materials and, without a word, decamped into the interior. He did not return that day, that night, or the next day, or the next night.

"Say, don't you think we ought to go after him," Billy said again and again, "something may have happened."

And, "No!" Honey always answered. "Trust that Dogan to take care of himself. You can't kill him."

Pete worked gradually across the island to the other side. There the beach was slashed by many black, saw-toothed reefs. The sea leaped up upon them on one side and the trees bore down upon them on the other. The air was filled with tumult, the hollow roar of the waves, the strident hum of the pines. For the first day, Pete entertained himself with exploration, clambering from one reef to another, pausing only to look listlessly off at

the horizon, climbing a pine here and there, swinging on a bough while he stared absently back over
the island. But although his look fixed on the
restless peacock glitter of the sea, or the moveless
green cushions that the massed trees made, it was
evident that it took no account of them; they
served only the more closely to set his mental gaze
on its half-seen vision.

The second morning, he arose, bathed, break-
fasted, lay for an hour in the sun; then drew pencil
and paper from his pack. He wrote furiously. If
he looked up at all, it was only to gaze the more
fixedly inwards. But mainly his head hung over
his work.

In the midst of one of these periods of absorption, a flower fell out of the air on his paper.
It was a brilliant, orange-colored tropical bloom,
so big and so freshly plucked that it dashed his
verse with dew. For an instant he stared stupidly
at it. Then he looked up.

Just above him, not very high, her green-and-
gold wings spread broad like a butterfly's, floated
Clara. Her body was sheathed in green vines, deli-

cately shining. Her hair was wreathed in fluttering yellow orchid-like flowers, her arms and legs wound with them. She was flying lower than usual. And, under her wreath of flowers, her eyes looked straight into his.

Pete stared at her stupidly as he had stared at the flower. Then he frowned. Deliberately he dropped his eyes. Deliberately he went on writing.

Whir-r-r-r-r! Pete looked up again. Clara was beating back over the island, a tempest of green-and-gold.

Again, he concentrated on his work.

Pete wrote all the rest of the day and by fire-light far into the night. He wrote all the next morning. In the middle of the afternoon, a sea-shell struck his paper, glanced off.

It was Clara again.

This time, apparently, she had come from the ocean. Sea-kelp, still glistening with brine, encased her close as with armor. A little pointed cap of kelp covered her tawny hair as with a helmet.

That gave her a piquant quality of boyishness. She was flying lower than he had ever seen her, and as Pete's eyelids came up she dropped nearer, threw herself into one of her sinuous poses, arms and legs outstretched close, hands and feet cupped, wrists, ankles, hips, shoulders all moving. She looked straight down into Pete's eyes; and this time she smiled.

Pete stared for another long moment. Then as though summoning all his resolution, he withdrew his eyes, nailed them to his paper. Clara peppered him with shells and pebbles; but he continued to ignore her. He did not look up again until a whir-r-r-r-r—loud at first but steadily diminishing—apprised him of her flight.

Pete again wrote the rest of the day and by firelight far into the night. In the middle of the morning he stopped suddenly, weighted his paper down with a stone, rolled over on to the pine-needles, and fell immediately into a deep sleep. He lay for hours, his face down, resting on his arm.

Whir-r-r-r-r!

Pete awoke with a start. His manuscript was gone. He leaped to his feet, stared wildly about. Not far off Clara was flying, almost on the ground. As he watched, she ascended swiftly. She held his poem in her hands. She studied it, her head bent. She did not once look up or back; her eyes still jealously glued to the pencil-scratchings, she drifted out to sea, disappeared.

Pete did not move. He watched Clara intently until she melted into the sky. But as he watched, his creative mood broke and evaporated. And suddenly another emotion, none the less fiercely ravaging, sluiced the blood into his face, filled his eyes with glitter, shook him as though a high wind were blowing, sent him finally speeding at a maniacal pace over the reefs.

"Say, do you think we'd better organize a search-party?" Honey asked finally.

"Not yet," said Ralph, "here he comes."

Pete was running down the trail like a deer. "I've finished my poem," he yelled jubilantly.

" Every last word of it. And now, boys," he added briskly before they could recover their breath, " I'm with you on this capture question."

For an instant, the others stared and blinked. " What do you mean, Pete? " Honey asked stupidly, after an instant.

" Well, I'm prepared to go as far as you like."

" But what changed you? " Honey persisted.

" Oh, hang it all," Pete said and never had his little black, fiery Irish face so twisted with irritation, so flamed with spirit, " a poet's so constituted that he's got to have a woman round to read his verse to. I want to teach Clara English so she can hear that poem."

There was a half-minute of silence. Then his listeners broke into roars. " You damned little mick you! " Honey said. He laughed at intervals for an hour.

They immediately broke the news of Pete's desertion to Merrill. Frank received it without any appearance of surprise. But he announced, with a sudden boom of authority in his big voice, that he expected them all to stand by their agreement.

Billy answered for the rest that they had no intention of doing anything else. But the four were now in high spirits. Among themselves, they no longer said, "If we capture them," but "When we capture them."

The stress of the situation at once pulled Frank away from his books. Again he took complete charge of the little group. He was a natural disciplinarian, as they had learned at the time of the wreck. Now his sense of responsibility developed a severity that was almost austerity. He kept them constantly at work. In private the others chafed at his tone of authority. But in his presence they never failed of respect. Besides, his remarkable unselfishness compelled their esteem, a shy vein of innocent, humorless sweetness their affection. "Old Frank" they always called him.

One afternoon, Frank started on one of the long walks which latterly he had abandoned. He left three of his underlings behind. Pete painted a water-color; Clara, weaving back and forth, watched his progress. Ralph worked on the big cabin—they called it the Clubhouse—Peachy whirling back and forth in wonderful air-patterns for his benefit. A distant speck of silver indicated Julia; Billy must be on the reef. Honey had left camp fifteen minutes before for the solitary afternoon tramp that had become a daily habit with him.

Frank's path lay part-way through the jungle. For half an hour he walked so sunk in thought that he glanced neither to the right nor the left. Then he stopped suddenly, held by some invisible, intangible, impalpable force. He listened. The air hummed delicately, hummed with an alien element, hummed with something that was neither the susurrus of insects nor the music of birds. He moved onward slowly and quietly. The hum grew and strengthened. It became a sound. It divided into component parts, whistlings, trillings, twitterings, callings. Bird-like they were—but they could come only from the human throat. Impersonal they were—and yet they were sexed, female and male. Frank looked about him carefully. A little distance away, the trail sent off a tiny feeler into the jungle. It dipped into one of the pretty glades which diversified the flatness of the island. Creeping slowly, Frank followed the sound.

Half-way down the slope, Honey Smith was standing, staring upwards. In his virile, bronzed semi-nudity, he might have been a god who had emerged for the first time into the air from the woods at his back. His lips were open and from them came sound.

Above him, almost within reach, Lulu floated, gazing downward. She had a listening look; and she listened fascinated. She seemed to lie motionless on the air. It was the first time that Merrill had seen Lulu so close. But in some mysterious way he knew that there was something abnormal about her. Her piquant Kanaka face shone with a strange emotion. Her narrow eyes were big with wonder; her blood-red lips had trembled open. She stared at Honey as if she were seeing him from a new angle. She stared, but sound came from her parted lips.

It was Honey who whistled and called. It was Lulu who twittered and trilled. No mating male bird could have put more of entreating tenderness into his voice. No mating female bird could have answered with more perplexity of abandon.

For a moment Frank stared. Then, with a sudden sense of eavesdropping, he moved noiselessly back until he struck the main trail.

He kept on until he came to the shady side of his favorite reef. He took from his pocket a book and began to read. To his surprise and discomfort, he could not get into it. Something psychological kept coming between him and the printed page. He tried to concentrate on a paragraph, a sentence, a phrase. It was like eating granite. It was like drinking dust. He stared at the words, but they seemed to float off the page.

That, then, was what all the other four men were doing while he was reading and writing, or while, with narrowed, scrutinizing eyes, he followed Chiquita's languid flight. He had not seen Chiquita for a week; he had been so busy getting the first part of his monograph into shape that he had not come to the reef. And all that week, the other men had been—— A word from the university slang came into his mind—twosing—came into it with a new significance. How descriptive that word was! How concrete! *Twosing!*

He took up his book again. He glued his eyes to the print. Five minutes passed; he was gazing at the same words. But now instead of floating off the page, they engaged in little dances, dizzyingly concentric. Suddenly something that was not of the mind interposed another obstacle to concentration, a jagged, purple shadow.

It was Chiquita.

Frank leaped to his feet and stood staring. The quickness of his movement—ordinarily he moved measuredly—frightened her. She fluttered, drifted away, paused. Frank stiffened. His immobility reassured her. She drifted nearer. Something impelled Frank to hold his rigid pose. But, for some unaccustomed reason, his hand trembled. His book dropped noiselessly on to the soft grass.

Chiquita floated down, closer than ever before.

She had undoubtedly just waked up. The dew of dreams still lay on her luscious lips and in her great black eyes. Scarlet flowers, flat-petaled, black-stamened, wreathed her dusky hair. Scarlet bands outlined her dusky shoulders. Scarlet streamers trailed in her wake. Never had she seemed more lazy and languid, more velvety and voluptuous, more colorful and sumptuous.

Frank stared and stared. Then, following an inexplicable impulse, he whistled as he had heard Honey whistle; and called as he had heard Honey call, the plaintive, entreating note of the mating male bird.

The same look which had come into Lulu's face came into Chiquita's, a look of wonder and alarm and—— She trembled, but she sank slowly, head foremost like a diver.

Frank continued softly to call and whistle. After an interval, another mysterious instinct impelled him to stop. Chiquita's lips moved; from them came answering sound, faint, breathy, scarcely voiced but exquisitely musical, exquisitely feminine, the call of the mating female bird.

When she stopped, Frank took it up. He raised his hand to her gently. As if that gave her confidence, she floated nearer, so close that he could

have touched her. But some new wisdom taught
him not to do that. She sank lower and lower
until she was just above him. Frank did not move
—nor speak now. She fluttered and continued to
sink. Now he could look straight into her eyes.
Frank had never really looked into a woman's eyes
before. The depth of Chiquita's was immeasur-
able. There were dreams on the surface. But his
gaze pierced through the dreams, through layer on
layer of purple black, to where stars lay. Some
emotion that constantly grew in her seemed to
melt and fuse all these layers; but the stars still
held their shine.

Slowly still, but as though at the urge of a compelled abandon, Chiquita sank lower and lower.
Nearer she came and nearer. The pollen from
the flowers at her breast sifted on to his face.
Now their eyes were level. And now——

She kissed him.

Billy, Ralph, and Pete sat on the sand banter-
ing Honey, who had returned in radiant spirits
from his walk.

" Here comes old Frank," Billy said. " He's running. But he's staggering. By George, I should think he was drunk."

Frank was drunk, but not with wine. When he came nearer, they saw that his face was white.

" You're right boys," he said quietly, " and I'm wrong." For a moment, he added nothing; but they knew what he meant. " A situation like this is special; it requires special laws. It's the masculine right of eminent domain. I give my consent —I—I—I—I agree to anything you want to do."

IV

"THE question before the house now is," said Ralph, "how are we going to do it? Myself, I'd be strong for winging them sometime when they're flying low."

The other four men burst into shocked remonstrance.

"Well, don't go up in the air," Ralph said in an amused voice. "It wouldn't hurt them any. And it seems to me if we've definitely made up our minds to capture them, the best way is the swiftest and surest."

"But to shoot a woman!" Pete exclaimed.

"Well, don't worry," Ralph answered him, "we haven't any guns. I did think of bows and arrows, though." He said this in the tone of one who throws out a suggestion and he stopped to study the faces of his fellow conspirators. Equally they expressed horror and disgust. "All right," he said with equanimity. " I see you're like all human nature. You're determined to pull off this cave-man stunt, but you want to do it with every appearance of chivalry and generosity. You're saving face. All right! I'm agreeable—although personally I think the quickest way the most merciful. Has anybody a better plan? "

Nobody had. It was obvious, though, from the talk that followed, that they had all been secretly considering the matter.

" The only thing for us to do," Honey said at once, " is to lie in wait. Conceal ourselves in the bushes and leap out on them."

" That sounds easy," Ralph said. " But has it occurred to you that these girls have the ears of wild animals? Has it occurred to you that they have all the instincts and cunning of the animal and all the intuition and prescience of the woman? Has it occurred to you that they always approach from above? "

" The only thing I can think of," said Billy, " is to lasso them. Only we've got to get them to alight and walk round first. But either they can't walk

or they don't like to walk. We must offer
them some bait.   Now, what in thunder would
tempt a creature that's one-third woman, one-third
bird, and one-third angel to come down to
earth? "

For a moment they were all silent considering
this question.   " By Jove," Ralph burst out finally,
" what are we all sitting here like dopes for?
Those trunks are full of women's clothes.   Did you
ever see a woman yet who wouldn't fall for ribbons and laces? "

" Good shot! " exclaimed Honey.   " Let's go
through the women-truck to-morrow and pick out
some things that would please a girl.   We'll put
them on the beach a good distance off from us, so
they'll not think it's a trap.   If we do that every
day for a week or two they'll get accustomed to
walking round while we're working.   It's our play
to take no notice of them whatever."

" That's the answer," Ralph said in a tone of
satisfaction.

Immediately after breakfast, the next morning,
they made for the file of trunks so contemptuously

rejected the first week of their stay. Honey, who was always head and shoulders in front of the others, broke open the first one.

"By jiminy, boys!" he shouted, seizing something that lay on top and waving it over his head, "we've got them on the go-off. By George," he went on, lowering his voice, "I bet that belonged to some darned pretty woman."

The men crowded about him; and, as they examined his find, their faces softened. Nothing could more subtly have emanated femininity. It was a hand-mirror of silver. Two carved Cupids held the glass between them. Their long wings made the handle.

"Put it down there on the hard sand," Ralph said, "where they can't fail to see it."

"Hold!" exclaimed Honey in a tone of burlesque warning. "There must be five mirrors. He knows nothing of women who thinks that one mirror may be divided among five girls. I hope Lulu cops this one."

His companions did not laugh. Apparently they were impressed with the sapience of his remark.

They searched the trunks until they had gathered the five that Honey demanded. They placed them in a row just above the high-water line. The mirrors caught the sunlight, reflected it.

"They won't do a thing to those girls," said Honey. There was the glee in his voice of a little boy who is playing a practical joke.

The girls came in a group in the middle of the afternoon.

"They've spotted them already," said Honey. "Trust a woman and a looking-glass."

The discovery ruined discipline; it broke ranks; the five girls flew high, flew low, flew separated, flew grouped, crowded about Julia, obviously asking her advice. Obviously she gave it; for following her quick, clear tones of advice came a confused chattering—remonstrance. Then Peachy, Clara, Chiquita, and Lulu dropped a little. Julia alone came no nearer. She alone showed no excitement.

The men meantime watched. They could not, as they had so loftily resolved, pretend to ignore the situation. But they kept silent and still. Once or twice the girls glanced curiously in their direction. But in the main they ignored them. Descending in big, slow, cautious, sliding curves, they circled nearer and nearer the sand.

Suddenly Lulu screamed. Still screaming, she bounded—it was almost that she bounced—straight up. The others streamed to the zenith in the wake of her panic, caught up, closed about her. There floated down the shrillness of agitated question and answer.

"What the Hades——" Ralph said in a mystified tone.

"I've got it," said Honey. "She caught a look at herself in one of the mirrors and she's scared. Don't be afraid, Lulu," he called in a reassuring tone; "it won't hurt you."

Lulu evidently got what he intended to convey. Again she sank slowly, hovered an instant close to the sand, brought her face near to a mirror, bounced up, dipped down, brought her face nearer, fluttered, put out one hand, withdrew it, put out the other, withdrew it, put out both, seized a mirror firmly, darted to the zenith.

"Well, what do you know about that!" said Billy. And, "Oh, the angels!" exclaimed Pete. Ralph's face opened in the fatuous grin which always meant satisfaction with him. Honey turned somersaults of delight. Even Frank twinkled.

For, high up in the heaven, five heads positively bumped over the meager oval of silver.

Lulu finally pulled out of the crowd and flew away. But all the time she held the mirror straight before her, clasped tightly in two hands, ecstatically "eating herself up" as Honey described it.

The men continued to watch.

Gradually, one after another, the other four girls fell under the lure of their vanity and their acquisitiveness.

Clara dove first, clutched a long-handled oval of yellow celluloid. Next Chiquita swam lazily downward, made a brief scarlet flutter on the beach, seized an elaborate double mirror set in gilded wood. Peachy followed; she chose a heart-shaped glass, ebony-framed. Last of all, Julia came floating slowly down. She took the only one that was left: it was, of course, the smallest; it was framed in carved ivory.

For the next ten minutes, the sky presented a picture of five winged women, stationed at various points of the compass, ecstatically studying their own beautiful faces in mirrors held in their white, strong-looking hands.

Then, flying together again, they discovered that the mirrors reflected. At first, this created panic, then amusement. Ensued a delicious girl-frolic. Darting through the air, laughing, jabbering, they played tag, throwing the light into each other's eyes. A little later Peachy gathered them into a bunch and whispered instructions. Immediately they began flashing the mirrors into the men's faces. To escape this bombardment, their victims had finally to throw themselves face downward on the sand.

In the midst of this excitement came disaster. Lulu dropped her mirror.

It hit square and shattered on the sand to many brilliant splinters. Lulu fell like a stone, seized the empty frame, gazed into it for a heart-broken second, burst into tears.

It was the first time that the men as a group had ever seen in the flying-girls an exhibition of this feminine faculty. For a moment, they watched her, deeply interested, as though confronted by an unfamiliar phenomenon. Then Billy wriggled. " Say, stop her, somebody," he begged, " I hate to hear a woman cry."

" So do I," said Peter, his face twisted into creases of discomfort. " She's your girl, Honey. Stop her, for God's sake."

" How's he going to stop her, I'd like to know?" demanded Ralph. " We don't converse very fluently yet, you know."

" Well, I know how to stop her," said Honey, leaping up. " I say, Lulu," he called. " Stop that crying, that's a good girl. It makes us all sick. I'll find you another mirror in a moment."

Lulu did not stop crying. Perhaps she was not too primitive to realize that tears are the argument a woman negotiates best. She wailed and wept assiduously.

Honey, in the meantime, flew to the trunks. He dumped one after another; clothes flew from either energetic hand like gravel from a shovel. Suddenly he gave a yell of triumph and brandished—— It was cheap and brass-bound, but it reflected the sunlight as well as though it had been framed in massy gold.

"Here you are, Lulu!" he called. He ran down the beach and held it up to her. Lulu caught the reflection. She dropped sheer. In her eagerness, she took it from Honey's very hand. And as she seized it, a tear dropped on his upturned cheek. And as the tear dropped, her face broke into smiles.

"Well," exclaimed Ralph an instant later, "if I'd had any idea that they were angels and not females, this would settle the question for me. Good Lord! Well, you *have* got a temper, my lady."

It was of Julia he spoke.

For, descending slowly and deliberately, Julia hovered an instant above a big rock. Then, with a tremendous slashing impulse of a powerful arm, she hurled her mirror on it. She flew in a very frenzy of haste into the west.

The girls returned the next morning early.

" After the graft," Ralph commented cynically.

Honey had been rifling the trunks again. He walked down to the beach with an armful of fans, piled them there, returned to camp. The girls descended, eyed them, ascended, gathered together, talked, descended, ascended again.

" What's the row? " Billy asked.

" They don't know what they're for," said Pete. He ran down on to the beach, seized a fan of feathers, opened it, and stood fanning himself. Then he put it down and ran back.

He had hardly returned to the group of men when Chiquita swooped down and seized the fan that he had dropped. The feathers were the exact scarlet of her wings. She floated about, fanning herself slowly, her teeth flashing white in her dusky face.

" By jiminy, if she only had a mantilla, she'd be a Spanish angel," Billy commented whimsically.

The other girls dropped down after a while and seized a fan, or in Clara's case two, and Peachy's three. They sailed off into the west, fanning themselves slowly.

"Say, we've got to have our ammunition all ready the next time they come," said Ralph. "I bet they're here this afternoon. They've never had any of these lover-like little attentions, apparently. And they're falling for them so quick that it's fairly embarrassing. Pete, you'll have to be muck-raking this island before we get through."

In their search for what Honey called "bait," they came across a trunk filled with scarfs of various descriptions; gauze, satin, chiffon; embroidered, sequined, fringed; every color, fabric, and decoration; every shape and size. "Drummers' samples!" Honey commented.

"I tell you what we'll do now," Ralph suggested. "Put the first five scarfs on the beach where they can get them. But if they want any more, make them take them from our hands. Be careful, though, not to frighten them. One move in their direction and we'll undo everything we've accomplished."

As Ralph prophesied, the girls came again that day, but they waited until after sunset. It was full-moon night, however; the island was as white as day. They must have seen the gay-colored heaps from a distance; they pounced on them at once. The air resounded with cooings of delight. There was no doubt of it; the scarfs pleased them almost as much as the mirrors. Before the first flush of their delight had passed, Honey ran down the beach, bearing aloft a long, shimmering, white streamer. Ralph followed with a scarf of black and gold. Billy, Pete, and Frank joined them, each fluttering a brilliant silk gonfalon.

The girls drew away in alarm at first. Then they drew together for counsel. All the time the men stood quiet, waving their delicately hued spoils. One by one—Clara first, then Chiquita, Lulu, Peachy, Julia—they succumbed; they sank slowly. Even then they floated for a long while, visibly swinging between the desire for possession and the instinct of caution. But in the end each one of them took from her mate the scarf he held up to her. Followed the prettiest exhibition of flying that Angel Island had yet seen. The girls fastened the long gauzes to their heads and shoulders. They flicked and flitted and flittered, they danced and pirouetted and spun through the air, trailing what in the aqueous moonlight looked like mist, irradiated, star-sown.

"Well," said Ralph that night after the girls had vanished, "I don't see that this business of handing out loot is getting us anywhere. We can keep this up until we've given those harpies every blessed thing in the trunks. Then where are we? They'll have everything we have to give, and we'll be no nearer acquainted. We've got to do something else."

"If we could only get them down to earth— if we could only accustom them to walking about," Honey declared, "I'm sure we could rig up some kind of trap."

"But you can't get them to do that," Billy said. "And the answer's obvious. They can't walk. You see how tiny, and useless-looking their feet are. They're no good to them, because they've never used them. It never occurs to them apparently even to try to walk."

"Well, who would walk if he could fly?" demanded Pete pugnaciously.

"Well said, son," agreed Ralph, "but what are we going to do about it?"

"I'll tell you what we can do about it," said Frank quietly, "if you'll listen to me." The others turned to him. Their faces expressed varying emotions—surprise, doubt, incredulity, a great deal of amusement. But they waited courteously.

"The trouble has been heretofore," Frank went on in his best academic manner, "that you've gone at this problem in too obvious a way. You've appealed to only one motive—acquisitiveness. There's a stronger one than that—curiosity."

The look of politely veiled amusement on the four faces began to give way to credulity. "But how, Frank?" asked Billy.

"I'll show you how," said Frank. "I've been thinking it out by myself for over a week now."

There was an air of quiet certainty about Frank. His companions looked furtively at each other. The credulity in their faces changed to interest. "Go on, Frank," Billy said. They listened closely to his disquisition.

"What ever gave you the idea, Frank?" Billy asked at the end.

"The fact that I found a Yale spring-lock the other day," Frank answered quietly.

The next morning, the men arose at sunrise and went at once to work. They worked together on the big cabin—the Clubhouse—and they dug and hammered without intermission all day long. Half-way through the morning, the girls came flying in a group to the beach. The men paid no attention to them. Many times their visitors flew up and down the length of the crescent of white, sparkling sand, each time dropping lower, obviously examining it for loot. Finding none, they flew in a body over the roof of the Clubhouse, each face turned disdainfully away. The men took no notice even of this. The girls gath-

ered together in a quiet group and obviously discussed the situation. After a little parley, they
flew off. Later in the afternoon came Lulu alone.
She hovered at Honey's shoulder, displaying all
her little tricks of graceful flying; but Honey was
obdurate. Apparently he did not see her. Came
Chiquita, floating lazily back and forth over
Frank's head like a monstrous, deeply colored
tropical bloom borne toward him on a breeze.
She swam down close, floated softly, but Frank
did not even look in her direction. Came Peachy
with such marvels of flying, such diving and soaring, such gyrating and flashing, that it took super-
human self-control not to drop everything and
stare. But nobody looked or paused. Came
Clara, posturing almost at their elbows. Came
all save Julia, but the men ignored them equally.

"Gee," said Honey, after they had all disappeared, "that took the last drop of resolution
in me. By Jove, you don't suppose they'll get sore
and stay away for good?"

Frank shook his head.

Day by day the men worked on the Clubhouse;

they worked their hardest from the moment of sunrise to the instant of sunset. It was a square building, big compared with the little cabins. They made a wide, heavy door at one end and long windows with shutters on both sides. These were kept closed.

"Only one more day's work," Frank said at the end of a fortnight, "and then——"

They finished the Clubhouse, as he prophesied, the next day.

"Now to furnish it," Frank said.

They put up rough shelves and dressing-tables. They put in chairs and hammocks. Then, working secretly at night when the moon was full, or in the morning just after sunrise—at any time during the day when the girls were not in sight—they transferred the contents of a half a dozen women's trunks to the Clubhouse. They hung the clothes conspicuously in sight; they piled many small toilet articles on tables and shelves; they placed dozens of mirrors about.

"It looks like a sale at the Waldorf," Honey said as they stood surveying the effect. "To-morrow, we begin our psychological siege. Is that right, Frank?"

"Psychological siege is right," answered Frank with an unaccustomed gayety and an unaccustomed touch of slang.

In the meantime the girls had shown their pique at this treatment in a variety of small ways. Peachy and Clara made long detours around the island in the effort not to pass near the camp. Chiquita and Lulu flew overhead, but only in order to throw pebbles and sand down on the men while they were working.

Julia alone took no part in this feud. If she was visible at all, it was only as a glittering speck in the far-off reaches of the blue sky.

The next time the four girls approached the island, the men arose immediately from their work. With an ostentatious carelessness, they went into the Clubhouse. With an ostentatious carefulness, they closed the door. They stayed there for three hours.

Outside, the girls watched this maneuver in visible astonishment. They drew together and talked it over, flew down close to the Clubhouse, flew about it in circles, examined it on every side, made even one perilous trip across the roof, the tips of their feet tapping it in vicious little dabs. But flutter as they would, jabber as they would, the Clubhouse preserved a tomb-like silence. After a while they banged on the shutters and knocked against the door; but not a sound or movement manifested itself inside.

They flew away finally.

The next day the same thing happened—and the next—and the next.

But on the fourth day, something quite different occurred.

The instant the men saw the girls approaching, they carefully closed the door and windows of the Clubhouse, and then marched into the interior of the island. Close by the lake, there was a thick jungle of trees—a place where the branches matted together, in a roof-like structure, leaving a cleared space below. The men crawled into this shelter on their hands and knees for an eighth of a mile. They stayed there three hours.

The girls had followed this procession in an aircourse that exactly paralleled the trail. When the men disappeared under the trees, they came together in a chattering group, obviously astonished, obviously irritated. Hours went by. Not a thing stirred in the jungle; not a sound came from it. The girls hovered and floated, dipped, dove, flew along the edge of the lake close to the water, tried by looking under the trees, to get what was going on. It was useless. Then they alighted on the tree-tops and swung themselves down from branch to branch until they were as near earth as they dared to come. Again they peered and peeped. And again it was useless. In the end, flying and floating with the disconsolate air of those who kill time, they frankly waited until the men emerged from the jungle. Then, again the girls took up the airy course that paralleled the trail to the camp.

For two weeks the men rigidly followed a program. Alternately they shut themselves inside the Clubhouse and concealed themselves in the forest. They stayed the same length of

time in both places—never less than three
hours.

For two weeks, the girls rigidly followed a program. When the men retired to the Clubhouse,
they spent the three hours hovering over it, sometimes banging viciously with feet and hands
against the walls, sometimes dropping stones on
the roof. When the men retired to the jungle,
they spent the three hours beating about the
branches of the trees, dipping lower and lower
into the underbrush, taking, as time went on,
greater and greater risks. But, as in both cases,
the men were screened from observation, all their
efforts were useless.

Finally came a day with a difference. The men
retired to the forest as usual but, by an apparent
inadvertence, they left the door of the Clubhouse
open a crack.

As usual the girls followed the men to the
lake, but this time there was a different air about
them; they seemed to bubble with excitement.
The men crawled under the underbrush and

waited. The girls made a perfunctory search of the jungle and then, as at a concerted signal, they darted like bolts of lightning back in the direction of the camp.

"I think we've got them, boys," said Frank. There was a kind of Berserker excitement about him, a wild note of triumph in his voice and a white flare of triumph in his face. His breath came in excited gusts and his nostrils dilated under the strain.

"I'm sure of it," agreed Ralph. "And, by Jove, I'm glad. I've never had anything so get on my nerves as this chase." Ralph did, indeed, look worn. Haggard and wild-eyed, he was shaking under the strain.

"Lord, I'm glad—but, Lord, it's some responsibility," said Honey Smith. Honey was not white or drawn. He did not shake. But he had changed. Still radiantly youthful, there was a new look in his face—resolution.

"I feel like a mucker," groaned Billy. He lay face down on a heap of vines, his forehead pressed against the cool leaves. "But it is right," he added as one arguing fiercely with himself. "It is right. There's no other way."

"I feel like a white slaver," said Pete. He was unshaven and the black shadow of his beard contrasted sharply with the white set look in his face. "It's hell to live, isn't it? But the worst of it is, we must live."

"Time's up." Frank breathed these words on the long gust of his outgoing breath. "Now, don't go to pieces. Remember, it must be done."

One behind the other, they crawled through the narrow tunnel that they had cut into the underbrush—found the trail.

"Let's swim across the lake," Honey suggested; "I'm losing my nerve."

"Good idea," Billy said. They plunged into the water. Fifteen minutes later, they emerged on the other side, cool, composed, ready for anything.

The long trip back to the camp was taken almost in silence. Once in a while, a mechanical "That's a new bird, isn't it?" came from Billy and, a perfunctory "Look at that color," from Pete. Frank walked ahead. He towered above the others. He kept his eyes to the front. Ralph followed. At intervals, he pulled himself up and peered into the sky or dropped and tried to pierce the untranslatable distance; all this with the quiet, furtive, prowling movements of some predatory beast. Next came Honey, whistling under his breath and all the time whistling the same tune. Billy and Pete, walking side by side, tailed the procession. At times, those two caught themselves at the beginning of shuddering fits, but always by a supreme effort they managed to calm themselves.

They came finally to the point where the jungle-trail joined the sand-trail.

"There isn't one in sight," said Frank.

"They may have flown home," Honey said doubtfully.

"They're in the Clubhouse," said Ralph. And he burst suddenly into a long, wild cry of triumph. The cry was taken up in a faint shrill echo. From the distance came shrieks—women's voices—smothered.

" By God, we've got them," said Frank again.
And then a strange thing happened. Pete Murphy crooked his elbow up to his face and burst into hysterical weeping.

All this time, the men were moving swiftly towards the Clubhouse. As they approached, the sound inside grew in volume from a hum of terrified whisperings accented by drumming wings, to a pandemonium of cries and sobs and wails.

" They'll make a rush when we open the door, remember," Ralph reminded them. His eyes gleamed like a cat's.

" Yes, but we can handle them," said Frank. " There isn't much nerve left in them by this time."

" I say, boys, I can't stand this," burst out Billy. " Open the door and let them out."

Billy's words brought murmured echoes of approval from Pete and Honey.

" You've got to stand it," Frank said in a tone of command. He surveyed his mutinous crew with a stern look of authority.

"I can't do it," Honey admitted.

"I feel sick," Pete groaned.

Just then emerged from the pandemonium within another sound, curt and sharp-cut, the crash against the door of something heavy.

"That door won't stand much of that," Frank warned. "They'll get out before we know it."

The look of irresolution went like a flash from Billy's face, from Honey's, from Pete's. The look of the hunter took its place, keen, alert, determined, cruel.

"Keep close behind me," Frank ordered. "When I open the door, push in as quick as you can. They'll try to rush out."

Inside the vibrant drumming kept up. Mixed with it came screams more sharp with terror. There came another crash.

Frank pounded on the door. "Stand back!" he called in a quiet tone of authority as if the girls could understand. He fitted the key to the lock, turned it, pulled the door open, leaped over the two broken chairs on the threshold. The others followed, crowding close.

The rush that they had expected did not come.

Apparently at the first touch on the door, the girls had retreated to the farthest corner. They stood huddled there, gathered behind Julia. They stood close together, swaying, half-supporting each other, their pinions drooped and trailing, their eyes staring black with horror out of their white faces.

Julia, a little in front, stood at defiance. Her wings, as though animated by a gentle voltage of electricity, kept lifting with a low purring whirr. Half-way they struck the ceiling and dropped dead. The tiny silvery-white feathers near her shoulders rose like fur on a cat's back. One hand was clenched; the other grasped a chair. Her face was not terrified; neither was it white. It glowed with rage, as if a fire had been built in an alabaster vase.

All about on the floor, on chairs, over shelves lay the gauds that had lured them to their capture. Of them all, Julia alone showed no change. Below the scarlet draperies swathing Chiquita's

voluptuous outlines appeared the gold stockings and the high-heeled gold slippers which she
had tried on her beautiful Andalusian feet. Neck-
laces swung from her throat; bracelets covered
her arms; rings crowded her fingers. Lulu had
thrown about her leafy costume an evening cape
of brilliant blue brocade trimmed with ermine.
On her head glittered a boudoir-cap of web lace
studded with iridescent mock jewels. Over her
mail of seaweed, Clara wore a mandarin's coat—
yellow, with a decoration of tiny mirrors. Her
hair was studded with jeweled hairpins, combs;
a jeweled band, a jeweled aigrette. Peachy had
put on a pink chiffon evening gown hobbled in the
skirt, one shoulder-length, shining black glove, a
long chain of fire-opals. Out of this emerged
with an astonishing effect of contrast her gleaming pearly shoulders and her lustrous blue
wings.

An instant the two armies stood staring at each
other—at close terms for the first time. Then,
with one tremendous sweep of her arm, Julia threw
something over their heads out the open door. It

flashed through the sunlight like a rainbow rocket, tore the surface of the sea in a dazzle of sparks and colors.

"There goes five hundred thousand dollars," said Honey as the Wilmington "Blue" found its last resting-place. "Shut the door, Pete."

With another tremendous sweep of her magnificent arm, Julia lifted the chair, swung it about her head as if it were a whip, rushed—not running or flying, but with a movement that was both—upon the five men. Her companions seized anything that was near. Lulu wrenched a shelf from its fastenings.

The men closed in upon them.

Twenty minutes later, silence had fallen on the Clubhouse, a silence that was broken only by panted breathing. The five men stood resting. The five girls stood, tied to the walls, their hands pinioned in front of them. At intervals, one or the other of them would call in an agonized tone to Julia. And always she answered with words that reassured and calmed.

The room looked as if it had housed a cyclone. The furniture lay in splinters; the feminine loot lay on the floor, trampled and torn.

"I'd like to sit down," Ralph admitted. It was the first remark that any one of the men had made. "Lucky they can't understand me. I'd hate them to know it, but I'm as weak as a cat."

"No sitting down, yet," Frank commanded, still in his inflexible tones of a disciplinarian. "Open the door, Pete—get some air in here!" He knelt before a sea-chest which filled one corner of the room, unlocked it, lifted the cover. The sunlight glittered on the contents.

"My God, I can't," said Billy.

"I feel like a murderer," said Pete.

"You've got to," Frank said in a tone, growing more peremptory with each word. "*Now.*"

"That's right," said Ralph. "If we don't do it now, we'll never do it.'

Frank handed each man a pair of shears.

"I sharpened them myself," he said briefly.

Heads over their shoulders, the girls watched.

Did intuition shout a warning to them? As with one accord, a long wail arose from them, swelled to despairing volume, ascended to desperate heights.

" Now! " Frank ordered.

They had thought the girls securely tied.

Clara fought like a leopardess, scratching and biting.

Lulu struggled like a caged eagle, hysteria mounting in her all the time until the room was filled with her moans.

Peachy beat herself against the wall like a maniac. She shrieked without cessation. One scream stopped suddenly in the middle—Ralph had struck her on the forehead. For the rest of the shearing session she lay over a chair, limp and silent.

Chiquita, curiously enough, resisted not at all. She only swayed and shrugged, a look of a strange cunning in her long, deep, thick-lashed eyes. But of them all, she was the only one who attempted to comfort; she talked incessantly.

Julia did not move or speak. But at the first

touch of the cold steel on her bare shoulders, she fainted in Billy's arms.

An hour later the men emerged from the Club-house.

"I'm all in," Honey muttered. "And I don't care who knows it. I'm going for a swim." Head down, he staggered away from the group and zig-zagged over the beach.

"I guess I'll go back to the camp for a smoke," Frank said. "I never realized before that I had nerves." Frank was white, and he shook at inter-vals. But some strange spirit, compounded equally of a sense of victory and of defeat, flashed in his eyes.

"I'm going off for a tramp." Pete was sunken as well as ashen; he looked dead. "Do you suppose they'll hurt themselves pulling against those ropes?" he asked tonelessly.

"Let them struggle for a while," Ralph ad-vised. Like the rest of them, Ralph was exhausted-looking and pale. But at intervals he swaggered and glowed. With his strange, new air of triumph and his white teeth glittering through his dark mustache, he was more than ever like some huge predatory cat. "Serves them right! They've taken it out of us for three months."

Billy did not speak, but he swayed as he followed Frank. He fell on his bed when they reached the camp. He lay there all night motionless, staring at the ceiling.

There was a tiny spot of blood on one hand.

V

I

DAWN on Angel Island.

A gigantic rose bloomed at the horizon-line; half its satin petals lay on the iron sea, half on the granite sky. The gold-green morning star was fading slowly. From the island came a confusion of bird-calls.

Addington emerged from the Clubhouse. Without looking about him, he staggered down the path to the Camp. The fire was still burning. The other men lay beside it, moveless, asleep with their clothes on. They waked as his footsteps drew near. Livid with fatigue, their eyelids dropping in spite of their efforts, they jerked upright.

" How are they? " Billy asked.

" The turn has come," Ralph answered briefly. As he spoke he crumpled slowly into a heap beside the fire. " They're going to live."

The others did not speak; they waited.

" Julia did it. She had dozed off. Suddenly in the middle of the night, she sat upright. She was as white as marble but there was a light back of her face. And with all that wonderful hair falling down—she looked like an angel. She called to them one by one. And they answered her, one by one. You never heard—it was like little birds answering the mother-bird's call. At first their voices were faint and weak. But she kept encouraging them until they sat up—God, it was——"

Ralph could not go on for a while.

" She gave them a long talk—she was so weak —she had to keep stopping—but she went right on—and they listened. Of course I couldn't understand a word. But I knew what she said. In effect, it was: ' We cannot die. We must all live. We cannot leave any one of us here alone. Promise me that you will get well! ' She pledged them to it. She made them take an oath, one after the other. Oh, they were obedient enough. They took it."

He stopped again.

" That talk made the greatest difference.   After
it was all over, I gave them some water.   They
were different even then.   They looked at me—
and they didn't shrink or shudder.   When I handed
Julia the cup, she made herself smile.   God, you
never saw such a smile.   I nearly——" he paused.
" I all but went back to the cabin and cut my throat.
But the fight's over.   They'll get well.   They're
sleeping like children now."

" Thank God! " Merrill groaned.   " Oh, thank
God! "

" I've felt like a murderer ever since——" Billy
said.   He stopped and his voice leaped with a sudden querulousness.   " You didn't wake me up;
you've done double guard duty during the night,
Ralph."

" Oh, that's all right.   You were all in—I felt
that——"   Ralph stammered in a shamefaced
fashion.   " And I knew I could stand it."

" There's a long sleep coming to you, Ralph,"
Pete said.   " You've hardly closed your eyes this
week.   No question but you've saved their lives."

Lik

JOHN RAE 13

bles

II

Mid-morning on Angel Island.

The sun had mounted half-way to the zenith; sky and sea and land glittered with its luster. Like war-horses, the waves came ramping over the smooth, shimmering sand; war-horses with bodies of jade and manes of silver.

Pete floated inshore on a huge comber, ran up the beach a little way and sat down. Billy followed.

" I've come out just to get the picture," Pete explained.

" Same here," said Billy.

For an instant, both men contemplated the scene with the narrowed, critical gaze of the artist.

The flying-girls were swimming; and swimming with the same grace and strength with which formerly they flew. And as if inevitably they must take on the quality of the element in which they mixed, they looked like mermaids now, just as formerly they had looked like birds. They carried heads and shoulders high out of the water. Webs of sea-spume glittered on the shining hair and on the white flesh. One behind the other, they swam in rhythmic unison. Regularly the long, round, strong-looking right arms reached out of the water, bowed forward, clutched at the wave, and pulled them on. Simultaneously, the left arms reached back, pushed against the wave, and shot them forward. Their feet beat the water to a lather.

They were headed down the beach, hugging the shore. Swim as hard as they could, Honey and Frank managed but to keep up with them. Ralph overtook them only in their brief resting-periods. Further inshore, carried ceaselessly a little forward and then a little back, Julia floated; floated with an unimaginable lightness and yet, somehow, conserved her aspect of a creature cut in marble.

" I have never seen anything so beautiful in any art, ancient or modern," Billy concluded. " When those strange draperies that they affect get wet, they look like the Elgin marbles."

" If we should take them to civilization," was

Pete's answer, " the Elgin marbles would become a joke."

Billy spoke after a long silence. " It's been an experience that—if I were—oh, but what's the use? You can't describe it. The words haven't been invented yet. I don't mean the fact that we've discovered members of a lost species—the missing link between bird and man. I mean what's happened since the capture. It's left marks on me. I'll bear them until I die. If we abandoned this island—and them—and went back to the world, I could never be the same person. If I woke up and found it was a dream, I could never be the same person."

" I know," Pete said, " I know. I've changed, too. We all have. Old Frank is a god. And Honey's grown so that—— Even Ralph's a different man. Changed—God, I should say I had. It's not only given me a new hold on things I thought I'd lost—morality, ethics, religion even— but it's developed something I have no word for— the fourth dimension of religion, faith."

" It's their weakness, I think, and their depend-ence." Now it was less that Billy tried to translate Pete's thought and more that he endeavored to follow his own. " It puts it up to a man so. And their beauty and purity and innocence and simplicity——" Billy seemed to be ransacking his vocabulary for abstract nouns.

" And that sense you have," Pete broke in eagerly, " of molding a virgin mind. It gives you a feeling of responsibility that's fairly terrifying at times. But there's something else mixed up with it—the instinct of the artist. It's as though you were trying to paint a picture on human flesh. You know that you're going to produce beauty." Pete's face shone with the look of creative genius. " The production of beauty excuses any method, to my way of thinking." He spoke half to himself. " God knows," he added after a pause, " whatever I've done and been, I could never do or be again. Sometimes a man knows when he's reached the zenith of his spiritual development. I've reached mine. I think they're beginning to trust us," he added after another long interval, in which silently they contemplated the moving composition. Pete's tone had come back to its everyday accent.

" No question about it," Billy rejoined. " If I do say it as shouldn't, I think my scheme was the right one—never to separate any one of them from the others, never to seem to try to get them alone, and in everything to be as gentle and kind and considerate as we could."

" That look is still in their eyes," Pete said. He turned away from Billy and his face contracted. " It goes through me like a knife——— When that's gone———"

" It will go inevitably, Pete," Billy reassured him cheerfully. Suddenly his own voice lowered. " One queer thing I've noticed. I wonder if you're affected that way. I always feel as if they still had wings. What I mean is this. If I stand beside one of them with my eyes turned away I always get an impression that they're still there, towering above my head—ghosts of wings. Ever notice it ? "

"Oh, Lord, yes ! " Pete agreed. " Often. I hate it. But that will go, too. Here they come."

The bathers had turned; they were swimming up the beach. They passed Julia, who joined the procession, and turned toward the land. Stretched in a long line, they rode in on a big wave. Billy and Pete leaped forward. Assisted by the men, the girls tottered up the sand, gathered into a little group, talking among themsleves. Their wet draperies clung to them in long, sweeping lines; but they dried with amazing quickness. The sun grew hotter and hotter. Their transient flash of animation died down; their conversation gradually stopped.

Chiquita settled herself flat on the sand, the sunlight pouring like a silver liquid into the blue-black masses of her hair, her narrow brows, her thick eyelashes. Presently she fell asleep. Clara leaned against a low ledge of rock and spread her coppery mane across its surface. It dried almost immediately; she divided it into plaits and coils and wove it into an elaborate structure. Her fingers seemed to strike sparks from it; it coruscated. Julia lay on her side, eyes downcast, tracing with one finger curious tangled patterns in the sand. Her hair blew out and covered her body as with a silken, honey-colored fabric; the lines of her figure were lost in its abundance. Peachy sat drooped over, her hand supporting her chin and her knees supporting her elbows, her eyes fixed on the horizon-line. Her hair dried, too, but she did not touch it. It flowed down her back and spread into a pool of gold on the sand. She might have been a mermaid cast up by that sea on which she gazed with such a tragic wistfulness—and forever cut off from it.

A little distance from the rest, Honey sat with Lulu. She was shaking the brown masses of her hair vigorously and Honey was helping her. He was evidently trying to teach her something because, over and over again, his lips moved to form two words, and over and over again, her red lips parted, mimicking them. Gradually, Lulu lost all interest in her hair. She let it drop. It floated like a furry mantle over her shoulders. Into her little brown, pointed face came a look of overpowering seriousness, of tremendous concentration. Occasionally Honey would stop to listen to her;

but invariably her recital sent him into peals of laughter. Lulu did not laugh; she grew more and more serious, more and more concentrated.

The other men talked among themselves. Occasionally they addressed a remark to their captives. The flying-girls replied in hesitating flutters of speech, a little breathy *yes* or *no* whenever those monosyllables would serve, an occasional broken phrase. Superficially they seemed calm, placid even. But if one of the men moved suddenly, an uncontrollable panic overspread their faces.

Honey arose after a long interval, strolled over to the main group.

" I think they're coming to the conclusion that we're regular fellows," he declared cheerfully. "Lulu doesn't jump or shriek any more when I run toward her."

" Oh, it's coming along all right," Frank said. " It's surprising how quickly and how correctly they're getting the language."

" I'm going to begin reading aloud to them

next week," Pete announced. "That'll be a picnic."

"It's been a long fight," Ralph said contentedly. "But we've won out. We've got them going. I knew we would." His eyes went to Peachy's face, but once there, their look of triumph melted to tenderness.

"What are we going to read them?" Honey asked idly. He did not really listen to Pete's answer. His eyes, sparkling with amusement, had gone back to Lulu, who still sat seriously practising her lesson. Red lips, little white teeth, slender pink tongue seemed to get into an inextricable tangle over the simple monosyllables.

"Leave that to me!" Pete was saying mysteriously. "I'll have them reading and writing by the end of another two months."

"It's curious how long it's taken them to get over that terror of us," said Billy. "I cannot understand it."

"Oh, they'll explain why they've been so afraid," said Frank, "as soon as they've got enough vocabulary. We cannot know, until they tell us how many of their conventions we have broken, how brutal we may have seemed."

"And yet," Billy went on, "I should think they'd see that we wouldn't do anything that wasn't for their own good. Well, just as soon as I can put it over with them, I'm going to give them a long spiel on the gentleman's code. I don't believe they'll ever be frightened of us again. Hello!"

Lulu had tottered over to their group, supporting herself by the ledge of rock. She pulled herself upright, balancing precariously. She put her sharp little teeth close, parted her lips and produced:

"K-K-K-K-K-K-KISS-S-S-S-S-S-S ME!"

The men brust into roars of laughter. Lulu looked from one face to the other in perplexity. In perplexity, the other women looked from her to them and at each other.

"Sounds like the Yale yell!" Pete commented.

"But what I can't understand," Billy said, reverting to his thesis, "is that they don't realize instantly that we wouldn't hurt them for anything—that that's a thing a fellow couldn't do."

III

Twilight on Angel Island.

The stars were beginning to shoot tiny white, five-pointed flames through the purple sky. The fireflies were beginning to cut long arcs of gold in the sooty dusk. The waves were coming up the low-tide beach with a long roar and retreating with a faint hiss. Afterwards floated on the air the music of the shingle, hundreds of pebbles pattering with liquid footsteps down the sand. Peals of laughter, the continuous bass roar of the men, an occasional uncertain soprano lilting of the women, came from the group. The girls were reciting their lessons.

> "Three little girls from school are we,
> Pert as schoolgirls well can be,
> Filled to the brim with girlish glee,
> Three little maids from school!"

intoned Lulu, Chiquita, and Clara together.

"Mary, Mary, quite contrary,
How does your garden grow?
Silver bells and cockle shells,
And pretty maids all in a row."

said Peachy.

" The hounds of spring are on winter's traces," began Julia. With no effort of the memory, with a faultless enunciation, a natural feeling for rhythm and apparently with comprehension, she recited the Atalanta chorus.

" That's enough for lessons," Honey demanded. " Wait a moment! "

He rushed into the bushes and busied himself among the fire-flies. The other four men, divining his purpose, joined him. They came back with handkerchiefs tied full of tiny, wriggling, fluttering green creatures.

In a few moments, the five women sat crowned with carcanets of living fire.

" Now read us a story," Lulu begged.

Pete drew a little book from his pocket. Discolored and swollen, the print was big and still black.

" ' Once upon a time,' " he began, " ' there was a little girl who lived with her father and her step-mother——' "

" What's ' stepmother '? " Lulu asked.

Pete explained.

" ' The stepmother had two daughters, and all three of these women were cruel and proud——' "

" What's ' cruel and proud '? " Chiquita asked.

Pete explained.

" ' And so between the three the little girl had a very hard time. She worked like a slave all day long, and was never allowed to go out of the kitchen. The stepmother and the proud sisters used to go to balls every night, leaving the little girl alone. Because she was always so dusty and grimy from working over the fire, they called her Cinderella. Now, it happened that the country was ruled by a very handsome young prince——' "

" What's ' handsome young prince '? " Clara asked.

Pete explained.

" ' And all the ladies of the kingdom were in love with him.' "

"What's 'in love'?" Peachy asked.

Pete closed the book.

"Ah, that's a question," he said after an instant of meditation, "that will admit of *some* answer. Say, you fellers, you'd better come into this."

IV

Moonlight on Angel Island.

The sea lay like a carpet of silver stretched taut from the white line of the waves to the black seam of the sky. The land lay like a crumpled mass of silver velvet, heaped to tinselled brightness here, hollowed to velvety shadow there. Over both arched the mammoth silver tent of the sky. In the cleft in the rock on the southern reef sat Julia and Billy. Under a tree at the north sat Peachy and Ralph. Scattered in shaded places between sat the others. The night was quiet; but on the breeze came murmurs sometimes in the man's voice, sometimes in the woman's. Fragmentary they were, these murmurs, and inarticulate; but their composite was ever the same.

V

Sunrise on Angel Island.

In and out among the trees, wound a procession following the northern trail. First came Lulu, white-clad, serious, pale, walking with Honey. The others, crowned with flowers and carrying garlands, followed, serious and silent, the women clinging with both hands to the men, who supported their snail-like, tottering progress with one arm about their waists. On the point of the northern reef, a cabin made of round beach-stones fronted the ocean. It fronted the rising sun now and a world, all ocean and sky, over which lay a rose dawnlight. Still silent, the procession paused and grouped about the house. Frank Merrill stepped forward and placed himself in front of Honey and Lulu.

"We are gathered here this morning," Frank said in his deep academic voice, "to marry this man to this woman and this woman to this man. If there is any reason why you should not enter into the married state, pause before it is too late."

His voice came to a full stop. He waited. "If not, I pronounce you man and wife."

Silently still, the others placed their garlands and wreaths at the feet of the wedded pair. Turning, they walked slowly back over the trail.

VI

Midnight on Angel Island.

Julia sat alone on the stone bench at the door of the Honeymoon House. She gazed straight ahead out on a star-lighted sea, which joined a star-lighted sky and stretched in pulsating star-gleams to the end of space. She gazed straight out, but apparently she saw nothing. Her eyes were abstracted and her brow furrowed. Her shoulders drooped.

A man came bounding up the path.

"Has Ralph been here?" he asked curtly. Billy's face was fiery. His eyes blazed.

"He's been here," Julia answered immediately. "He's gone!"

"By God, I'll kill him!" Billy turned white.

Julia's brow smoothed. She smiled a little. "No, you will not kill him," she said with her old serene air. "You will not have to kill him. He will never come again."

"Did he try to make love to you?"

"Yes."

"How did he justify himself?"

"He appealed to me to save him. I did not quite understand from what. He said I could make a better man of him." Julia laughed a little. "How did you know he was here?"

"I stopped at their cabin. He was not there. Peachy did not know where he was. Of course, I guessed at once. I came here immediately."

"Did Peachy seem troubled?"

"No. She doesn't care. Pete was there, examining her drawings. They're half in love with each other. And then again, Pete doesn't know, or if he does know, he doesn't care, that Clara is doing her damnedest to start a flirtation with Honey. And Lulu has walked about like a woman in a dream for weeks. What are we all coming to? There's nothing but flirting here!"

"It must be so," Julia said, "as long as men and women are idle."

"But how can we be anything but idle? There's nothing to do on this island."

"I don't know," said Julia slowly; "I don't know."

"Julia," Billy said in a pleading voice, "marry me!"

A strange expression came into Julia's eyes. Part of it was irresolution and part of it was terror. But a poignant wistful tenderness fused both these emotions, shot them with light.

"Not yet," she said in a terrified voice. "Not yet!"

"Why?"

"I don't know—why. Only that I cannot."

"Then, when will you marry me? Julia, I see all the others together and it—— You don't know what it does to me."

"Yes, I know! It kills me too."

"Then why wait?"

"Because——" The poignant look went for an instant from Julia's eyes. A strange brooding came in its place. "Because a little voice inside says, 'Wait!'"

"Julia, do you love me?"

Julia did not answer. She only looked at him.

"You are sure there is nobody else?"

"I am sure. There could never be anybody else—after that first night when I waked you from sleep."

"It is forever, then?"

"Forever."

Billy sighed. "I'll wait, then—until eternity shrivels up."

They sat for a long time, silent.

"Here comes somebody," Billy said suddenly. "It's one of the girls," he added after a moment of listening. "I'll leave you, I guess."

He melted into the darkness.

A woman appeared, dragging herself along by means of the rail. It was Lulu, a strange Lulu, a Lulu pallid and silent, but a Lulu shining-eyed. She pulled herself over to Julia's side. "Julia!" Julia! Oh, Julia!"

Lulu's voice was not voice. It was not speech.

Liquid sound flowed from her lips, crystallizing at the touch of the air, to words. " Julia, I came to you first, after Honey. I wanted you to know."

" Oh, Lulu," Julia said, " not——"

Her eyes reflected the stars in Lulu's eyes. And there they stood, their two faces throwing gleam for gleam.

" Yes," said Lulu. Suddenly she knelt sobbing on the floor, her face in Julia's lap.

VII

Mid-afternoon on Angel Island.

Four women sat in the Honeymoon House, sewing. Outside the world still lay in sunshine, the land cut by the beginning of shadow, the sea streaked with purple and green.

" Why didn't you bring the children? " Julia asked.

Lulu answered. " Honey and Frank were going in swimming this morning, and they said they'd take care of them. I'm glad to get Honey-Boy off my hands for an afternoon."

" And why hasn't Peachy come? " Julia asked.

" I stopped as I went by," Lulu explained. " Oh, Julia, I wish you didn't live way off here— it takes us an hour of crawling to pull ourselves along the path. Angela hadn't waked up yet. It was a longer nap than usual. Peachy said she'd come just as soon as she opened her eyes. I went in to look at her. Oh, she's such a darling, smiling in her sleep. Oh, I do hope I have a girl-baby sometime."

" I do, too," said Clara. " Peterkin's fun, of course. But I can't do the things for a boy that I could for a girl."

" I'd rather have boys," Chiquita said; " they're less trouble."

" Would you rather have boys or girls, Julia? " Lulu asked.

" Girls! " said Julia decisively. " A big family of girls."

" Then," Lulu began, and a question trembled in her bright eyes and on her curved lips.

But, " Here's Peachy! " Julia exclaimed before she could go on.

Peachy came toiling up the path, pulling herself along, both hands on the wooden rail. She tottered, but in spite of her snail-like progress, it was evident that she hurried. A tiny bundle hung between her shoulders. It oscillated gently with her haste.

"Let me take Angela," Julia said as Peachy struggled over the threshold.

"Wait!" Peachy panted. She sank on a couch.

There was a strange element in her look, an overpowering eagerness. This eagerness had brimmed over into her manner; it vibrated in her trembling voice, her fluttering hands. She sat down. She reached up and lifted the baby from her shoulders to her lap. Angela still slept, a delicate bud of a girl-being. But Peachy gave her audience no time to study the sleeping face. She turned the baby over. She pulled the single light garment off. Then she looked up at the other women.

The little naked figure lay in the golden sunlight, translucent, like an angel carved in alabaster. But on the shoulder-blades lay shadow, deep shadow—no, not shadow, a fluff of feathery down.

"Wings!" Peachy said. "My little girl is going to fly!"

"Wings!" the others repeated. "Wings!"

And then the room seemed to fill with tears that ended in laughter, and laughter that ended in tears.

VI

"THEY won't be home until very late to-night," announced Lulu. "The work they're doing now is hard and irritating and fussy. Honey says that they want to get through with it as soon as possible. He said they'd keep at it as long as the light lasted."

"It seems as if their working days grew longer all the time," Clara said petulantly. "They start off earlier and earlier in the morning and they stay later and later at night. And did you know that they are planning soon to stay a week at the New Camp—they say the walk back is so fatiguing after a long day's work."

The others nodded.

"And then the instant they've had their dinner," Lulu continued, "off they go to that tiresome Clubhouse—for tennis and ball and bocci. It seems, somehow, as if I never had a chance to

talk with Honey nowadays. I should think they'd
get enough of each other, working side by side all
day long, the way they do. But no! The moment
they've eaten and had their smoke, they must get
together again. Why is it, I wonder? I should
think they would have said all they had to say in
the daytime."

"Pete is worse than any of them," Clara went
on. "After he comes back from the Clubhouse,
he wants to sit up and write for an hour or two.
Oh, I get fairly desperate sometimes, sitting there
listening to the eternal scratching of his pen. I
cannot understand his point of view, to save my
life. If I talk, it irritates him. My very breathing annoys him; he cannot have me in the same
room with him. But if I leave the cabin, he can't
write a word. He wants me near, always. He says
it's the knowing I'm there that makes him feel
like writing. And then Sundays, if he isn't writing, he's painting. I don't mind his not being
there in the daytime in a way because, of course,
there's always Peterkin. But at night, when I've
put Peterkin to bed I do want something different

to happen.   As it is, I have to make a scene to get
up any excitement.   I do it, too, without compunc-
tion.   When it gets to the point that I know I must
scream or go crazy, I scream.   And I do a good job
in screaming, too."

"What would you like him to do, Clara?"
Julia asked.

The petulant frown between Clara's eyebrows
deepened.   "I don't know," she said wearily.   "I
don't know what it is that I want to do; but I want
to do something.   Peterkin is asleep and perfectly
safe—and I feel like going somewhere.   Now, if
I could fly, it would rest me so, to go for a long,
long journey through the air."   As she concluded,
some new expression, some strange hardness of
her maturity, melted; her face was for an instant
the face of the old Clara.

Julia made no comment.

It was Chiquita who took it up.

"My husband talks enough.   In fact, he talks
all the time. But if I tire of his voice, I let
myself fall asleep. He never notices. That is
why I've grown so big. Sometimes "—discontent

dulled for an instant the slow fire of her slumberous eyes—"sometimes my life seems one long sleep. If it weren't for Junior, I'd feel as if I weren't quite alive."

"Ralph talks a great deal," Peachy said listlessly, "by fits and starts, and he takes me out when he comes home, if he happens to feel like walking himself. He says, though, that it exhausts him having to help me along. But it isn't that I want particularly. Often I want to go out alone. I want to soar. The earth has never satisfied me. I want to explore the heights. I want to explore them alone, and I want to explore them when the mood seizes me. And I want to feel when I come back that I can talk about it or keep silent as he does. But I must make my discoveries and explorations in my own way. Ralph sometimes gives me long talks about astronomy—he seems to think that studying about the stars will quiet me. One little flight straight up would mean more to me than all that talk. Ralph does not understand it in me, and I cannot explain it to him. And yet he feels exactly that way himself—he's always going off by himself through unexplored trails on the island. But he cannot comprehend how I, being a woman, should have the same desire. Do you remember when our wings first began to grow strong and our people kept us confined, how we beat our wings against the wall—beat and beat and beat? At times now, I feel exactly like that. Why, sometimes I envy little Angela her wings."

The five women reclined on long, low rustic couches in the big, cleared half-oval that was the Playground for their children. It began—this half-oval—in high land among the trees and spread down over a beach to the waters of a tiny cove. Between the high tapering boles of the pines at their back the sky dropped a curtain of purple. Between the long ledges of tawny rock in front the sea stretched a carpet of turquoise. And between pines and sea lay first a rusty mat of pine-needles, then a ribbon of purple stones, then a band of glittering sand. In the air the resinous smell of the pines competed with the salty tang of the ocean. High up, silver-winged gulls curved and dipped and called their creaking signals.

At the water's edge four children were playing. Honey-Boy had waded out waist-deep. A sturdy, dark, strong-bodied, tiny replica of his father, he stood in an exact reproduction of one of Honey's poses, his arms folded over his little pouter-pigeon chest, lips pursed, brows frowning, dimples inhibited, gazing into the water. Just beyond, one foot on the bottom, Peterkin pretended to swim. Peterkin had an unearthly beauty that was half Clara's coloring—combination of tawny hair with gray-green eyes—and half Pete's expression—the look, doubly strange, of the Celt and the genius. Slender and beautifully formed, graceful, he was in every possible way a contrast to virile little Billy-Boy; he was even elegant; he had the look of a story-book prince. Far up the beach, cuddled in a warm puddle, naked, sat a fat, red-headed baby, Frank Merrill, Junior. He watched the others intently for a while. Then breaking into a grin which nearly bisected the face under the fiery thatch, he began an imitative paddle with his pudgy hands and feet.

Flitting hither and yon, hovering one moment at

the water's edge and another at Junior's side, moving with a capricious will-o'-the-wisp motion that dominated the whole picture, flew Angela.

Beautiful as the other children were, they sank to commonplaces in contrast with Angela.

For Angela was a being of faëry. Her single loose garment, serrated at the edges, knee-length, and armless, left slits at the back for a pair of wings to emerge. Tiny these wings were, and yet they were perfect in form; they soared above her head, soft, fine, shining, delicate as milkweed-down and of a white that was beginning, near the shoulders, to deepen to a pale rose. Angela's little body was as slender as a flower-stem. Her limbs showed but the faintest of curves, her skin but the faintest of tints. Almost transparent in the sunlight, she had in the shadow the coloring of the opal, pale rose-pinks and pale violet-blues. Her hair floated free to her shoulders; and that, more than any other detail, seemed to accent the quality of faëry in her personality. In calm it clung to her head like a pale-gold mist; in breeze it floated away like a pale-gold nimbus. It seemed as though a shake of her head would send it drifting off—a huge thistle-down of gold. Her eyes reflected the tint of whatever blue they gazed on, whether it was the frank azure of the sky or the mysterious turquoise of the sea. And yet their look was strangely intent. When she passed from shadow to sunshine, the light seemed to dissolve her hair and wing-edges, as though it were gradually taking her to itself.

"Oh, yes, Peachy," Lulu said, "Angela's wings must be a comfort to you. You must live it all over again in her."

"I do!" answered Peachy. "I do." There was tremendous conviction in her voice, as though she were defending herself from some silent accusation. "But it isn't the same. It isn't. It can't be. Besides, I want to fly with her."

The ripples in the cove grew to little waves, to big waves, to combers. The women talked and the children played. Honey-Boy and Peterkin waded out to their shoulders, dipped, and pretended to swim back. Angela flew out to meet a wave bigger than the others, balanced on its crest.

Wings outspread, she fluttered back, descended when the crash came in a shower of rainbow drops. She dipped and rose, her feathers dripping molten silver, flew on to the advancing crest.

"Oh," Lulu sighed, "I do want a little girl. I threatened if this one was a boy to drown it." "This one" proved to be a bundle lying on the pine-needles at her side. The bundle stirred and emitted a querulous protest. She picked it up and it proved to be a baby, just such another sturdy little dark creature as Honey-Boy must have been. "Your mother wouldn't exchange you for a million girls now," Lulu addressed him fondly. "I pray every night, though, that the next one will be a girl."

"I want a girl, too," Clara remarked. "Well, we'll see next spring." Clara had not been happy at the prospect of her first maternity, but she was jubilant over her second.

"It will be nice for Angela, too," Peachy said, "to have some little girl to play with. Come, baby!" she called in a sudden access of tenderness.

Angela flew down from the tip of a billow,

came fluttering and flying up the beach. Once or twice, for no apparent reason, her wings fell dead, sagged for a few moments; then her little pink, shell-like feet would pad helplessly on the sand. Twice she dropped her pinions deliberately; once to climb over a big root, once to mount a boulder that lay in her path. "Don't walk, Angela!" Peachy called sharply at these times. "Fly! Fly!" And obediently, Angela stopped, waited until the strength flowed into her wings, started again. She reached the group of mothers, not by direct flight, but a complicated method of curving, arching, dipping, and circling. Peachy arose, balanced herself, caught her little daughter in mid-air, kissed her. The women handed her from one to the other, petting and caressing her.

Julia received her last. She sat with Angela in the curve of her arm, one hand caressing the drooped wings. It was like holding a little wild bird. With every breeze, Angela's wings opened. And always, hands, feet, hair, feathers fluttered with some temperamental unrest.

The boys, tiring of the waves, came scrambling

in their direction. Half-way up the beach, they too came upon the boulder in the path. It was too high and smooth for them to climb, but they immediately set themselves to do it. Peterkin pulled himself half-way up, only immediately to fall back. Junior stood for an instant imitatively reaching up with his baby hands, then abandoning the attempt waddled off after a big butterfly. Honey-Boy slipped and slid to the ground, but he was up in an instant and at it again.

Angela fluttered with baby-violence. Julia opened her arms. The child leaped from her lap, started half-running, half-flying, caught a seaward-going breeze, sailed to the top of the boulder. She balanced herself there, gazing triumphantly down on Billy-Boy who, flat on his stomach, red in the face, his black eyes bulging out of his head, still pulled and tugged and strained.

"Honey-Boy's tried to climb that rock every day for three months," Lulu boasted proudly. "He'll do it some day. I never saw such persistence. If he gets a thing into his head, I can't do anything with him."

" Angela starts to climb it occasionally," Peachy
said. " But, of course, I always stop her. I'm
afraid she'll hurt her feet."

Above the rock stretched the bough of a big
pine. As she contemplated it, a look of wonder
grew in Angela's eyes, of question, of uncertainty.
Suddenly it became resolution. She spread her
wings, bounded into the air, fluttered upwards, and
alighted squarely on the bough.

" Oh, Angela! " Peachy called anxiously. Then,
joyously, " Look at my baby. She'll be flying as
high as we did in a few years. Oh, how I love to
think of that! "

She laughed in glee—and the others laughed
with her. They continued to watch Angela's
antics, their faces growing more and more gay.
Julia alone did not smile; but she watched the exhibition none the less steadily.

Three years had brought some changes to the
women of Angel Island; and for the most part they
were devastating changes. They were still wingless. They wore long trailing garments that concealed their feet. These garments differed in

color and decoration, but they were alike in one detail—floating, wing-like draperies hung from the shoulders.

Chiquita had grown so large as to be almost unwieldy. But her tropical coloring retained its vividness, retained its breath-taking quality of picturesqueness, retained its alluring languor. She sat now holding a huge fan. Indeed, since the day that Honey had piled the fans on the beach, Chiquita had never been without one in her hand. Scarlet, the scarlet of her lost pinions, seemed to be her color. Her gown was scarlet.

Lulu had not grown big, but she had grown round. That look of the primitive woman which had made her strange, had softened and sobered. Her *beauté troublante* had gone. Her face was the face of a happy woman. The maternal look in her eyes was duplicated by the married look in her figure. She was always busy. Even now, though she chattered, she sewed; her little fingers fluttered like the wings of an imprisoned bird. Indeed, she looked like a little sober mother-bird in her gray and brown draperies. She was the best housewife among them. Honey lacked no creature comfort.

Clara also had filled out; in figure, she had improved; her elfin thinness had become slimness, delicately curved and subtly contoured. Also her coloring had deepened; she was like a woman cast in gold. But her expression was not pleasant. Her light, gray-green eyes had a petulant look; her thin, red lips a petulant droop. She was restless; something about her moved always. Either her long slender fingers adjusted her hair or her long slender feet beat a tattoo. And ever her figure shifted from one fluid pose to another. She wore jewels in her elaborately arranged hair, jewels about her neck, on her wrists, on her fingers. Her green draperies were embroidered in beads. She was, in fact, always dressed, costumed is perhaps the most appropriate word. She dressed Peterkin picturesquely too; she was always studying the illustrations in their few books for ideas. Clara was one of those women at whom instinctively other women gaze—and gaze always with a question in their eyes.

Peachy was at the height of her blonde bloom; all pearl and gold, all rose and aquamarine. But something had gone out of her face—brilliance. And something had come into it—pathos. The look of a mischievous boy had turned to a wild gipsy look of strangeness, a look of longing mixed with melancholy. In some respects there was more history written on her than on any of the others. But it was tragic history. At Angela's birth Peachy had gone insane. There had come times when for hours she shrieked or whispered, " My wings! My wings! My wings! " The devoted care of the other four women had saved her; she was absolutely normal now. Her figure still carried its suggestion of a potential, young-boy-like strength, but maternity had given a droop, exquisitely feminine, to the shoulders. She always wore blue—something that floated and shimmered with every move.

Julia had changed little; for in her case, neither marriage nor maternity had laid its transmogrify-

ing touch upon her. Her deep blue-gray eyes—
of which the brown-gold lashes seemed like reeds
shadowing lonely lakes—had turned as strange as
Peachy's; but it was a different strangeness.
Her mouth—that double sculpturesque ripple of
which the upper lip protruded an infinitesimal frac-
tion beyond the lower one—drooped like Clara's;
but it drooped with a different expression. She
had the air of one who looks ever into the distance and broods on what she sees there. Perhaps because of this, her voice had deepened to
a thrilling intensity. Her hair was pulled straight
back to her neck from the perfect oval of her face.
It hung in a single, honey-colored braid, and it
hung to the very ground. She always wore white.

" Do you remember "—Chiquita began presently. Her lazy purring voice grew soft with tenderness. The dreamy, unthinking Chiquita of four
years back seemed suddenly to peer through the
unwieldy Chiquita of the present—" how we used
to fly—and fly—and fly—just for the love of flying? Do you remember the long, bright day-
flyings and the long, dark night-flyings? "

"And sometimes how we used to drop like stones until we almost touched the water," Lulu said, a sparkle in her cooing, friendly little voice. "And the races! Oh, what fun! I can feel the rush of the air now."

"Over the water." Peachy flung her long, slim arms upward and a delicious smile sent the tragedy scurrying from her sunlit face. "Do you remember how wonderful it was at sunset? The sky heaving over us, shot with gold and touched with crimson. The sea pulsing under us lined with crimson and splashed with gold. And then the sunset ahead—that gold and crimson hole in the sky. We used to think we could fly through it some day and come out on another world. And sometimes we could not tell where sea and sky joined. How we flew—on and on—farther each time—on and on—and on. The risks we took! Sometimes I used to wonder if we'd ever have the strength to get home. Yet I hated to turn back. I hated to turn away from the light. I never could fly towards the east at sunset, nor towards the west at sunrise. It hurt! I used to think,

when my time came to die, that I would fly out to
sea—on and on till I dropped."

"I loved it most at noon," Chiquita said, "when
the air was soft. It smelled sweet; a mixture of
earth and sea. I used to drift and float on great
seas of heat until I almost slept. That was wonderful; it was like swimming in a perfumed air or
flying in a fragrant sea."

"Oh, but the storms, Julia!" Lulu exclaimed.
A wild look flared in her face, wiped off entirely
its superficial look of domesticity. "Do you remember the heavy, night-black cloud, the thunder
that crashed through our very bodies, the lightning
that nearly blinded us, and the rain that beat us
almost to pieces?"

"Oh, Lulu!" Julia said; "I had forgotten
that. You were wonderful in a storm. How you
used to shout and sing and leap through the air
like a wild thing! I used to love to watch you;
and yet I was always afraid that you would hurt
yourself."

"I loved the moonlight most. I do now."
The petulance went out of Clara's eyes;

dreams came into its place. "The cool softness of the air, the brilliant sparkle of the stars! And then the magic of the moonlight! Young child-moon, half-grown girl-moon, voluptuous woman-moon, sallow, old-hag-moon, it was alike to me. Pete says I'm ' fey ' in the moonlight. He says I'm Irish then."

"I loved the sunrise," said Julia. "I used to steal out, when you girls were still sleeping, to fly by dawn. I'd go up, up, up. At first, it was like a huge dewdrop—that morning world—then, colder and colder—it was like a melted iceberg. But I never minded that cold and I loved the clear-ness. It exhilarated me. I used to run races with the birds. I was not happy until I had beaten the highest-flying of them all. Oh, it was so fresh and clean then. The world seemed new-made every morning. I used to feel that I'd caught the mo-ment when yesterday became to-day. Then I'd sink back through layer on layer of sunlight and warm, perfume-laden, dew-damp breeze, down, down until I fell into my bed again. And all the time the world grew warmer and warmer. And

I loved almost as well that instant of twilight when the world begins to fade. I used to feel that I'd caught the moment when to-day had become to-morrow. I'd fly as high as I could go then, too. Then I'd sink back through layer on layer of deepening dusk, while one by one the stars would flash out at me—down, down, down until my feet touched the water. And all the time the air grew cooler and cooler."

"My wings! My wings!" Peachy did not shriek these words with maniacal despair. She did not whisper them with dreary resignation. She breathed them with the rapture of one who looks through a narrow, dark tunnel to measureless reaches of sun-tinted cloud and sea.

"Do you remember the first time we ever saw them?" Lulu asked after a long time. This was obviously a deliberate harking back to lighter things. A gleam of reminiscence, both mischievous and tender, fired her slanting eyes.

The others smiled, too. Even Peachy's face relaxed from the look of tension that had come into it. "I often think that was the happiest time," she sighed, " those weeks before they knew we were here. At least, they knew and they didn't know. Ralph said that they all suspected that something curious was going on—but that they were so afraid that the others would joke about it, that no one of them would mention what was happening to him. Do you remember what fun it was coming to the camp when they were asleep? Do you remember how we used to study their faces to find out what kind of people they were? "

" And do you remember "—Chiquita rippled a low laugh—" how we would leap into the air if they stirred or spoke in their sleep? Once, Honey started to wake up—and we were off over the water before he could get his eyes open."

" Oh, but Honey told me that he heard us laugh that time," Lulu explained. " He told the men the next day and, oh, how they joked him."

" And then," Chiquita went on, " once Billy actually did wake up. You were bending over him, Julia. I remember we all kept as still as the dead. And you—oh, Julia, you were wonderful—you did not even breathe. He seemed to fade back into sleep again."

"He says now that I hypnotized him," Julia explained.

"Do you remember," Clara took it up, "that we even considered kidnapping one of them? If we'd known what to do with him, I think we might have tried it."

"Yes," said Chiquita. "But I think it was just as well we didn't. We wouldn't have carried it off well. There's something about them that's terrifying. Do you remember that time we saved Honey from the shark, how we trembled all the time we carried him through the air. He knew it, too—I noticed how triumphantly he smiled."

"Honey told me once"—Lulu lowered her voice—"that it was the fact that we trembled— that we seemed so much women, in spite of being creatures of the air—that made him determine to capture us."

"Well, there's something about them that weakens you," Chiquita said in a puzzled tone. "It's like a spell. At first I always felt quivery and trembly if I stood near them."

"It's power," Julia explained.

"I used even to be afraid of their voices," Chiquita went on.

"Oh, so was I," Lulu agreed. "I felt as I did when I heard thunder for the first time. It went through me. It made me shake. I was afraid, but I wanted to hear it again."

"Do you remember the first time we saw them *walk!*" Clara said. Her face twisted with the expression of a past loathing. "How it disgusted us! It seemed to me the most hideous motion I had ever seen—so unnatural, so ungraceful, so repellent. It took me a long time to get used to that. And as for their running——"

"It's curious how that feeling still lingers in us," exclaimed Peachy. "That contempt for the thing that walks. Occasionally Angela starts to imitate the boys—it seems as if I would fly out of my skin with horror. I shall always feel superior to Ralph, I know."

"Do you remember the first talks we ever had

after we'd got our first glimpse of them?" asked
Clara. "How astonished we were—and half
frightened and yet—in a queer way—excited and
curious?"

"And after we got over our fright," Lulu
carried the memories along, "and had made up
our minds we didn't care whether they discovered
us or not, what fun we had with them! How we
played over the entire island and yet it took them
such a long time to discover us."

"Oh, they're awfully stupid about seeing or
guessing things," Peachy said disdainfully. "My
mind always leaps way ahead of Ralph's."

"Do you remember that at first we used to have
regular councils," Lulu asked, "before—before——"

"Before we agreed each to go her own way,"
Peachy finished it for her.

"All of us pitted against you, Julia." Chiquita sighed. "I often think now, Julia, how you
used to talk to us. How you used to beg us not
to go to the island. How you argued with us!
The prophecies you made! They've all come true.

I can hear you now: "Don't go to the island.' 'Come away with me and we will fly back south before it is too late.' ' Come away while you can!' 'In a little while it will be too late.' 'In a little while I shall not be able to help you!'"

"And how we fought you, Julia!" Clara said. "How we denied everything you said, every one of us knowing in her heart that you were right!"

"But," Julia said, "later, I told you that I might not be able to help myself, and you see I wasn't."

"Did they ever guess that we had quarrelled, I wonder?" Clara asked.

"Yes," Lulu answered eagerly. "Honey guessed it. Now, wasn't that clever of him?"

"Not so very," Clara replied languidly. "I guessed that *they* had quarrelled. And I had a strong suspicion," she added consciously, "that it was about us."

"I wonder," Peachy said somberly, "what would have happened if we had taken Julia's advice."

"Are you sorry, Peachy?" Julia asked.

"No, I'm not sorry exactly," Peachy answered slowly. "I have Angela, of course. Are you sorry, Julia?"

"No," replied Julia.

"Julia," Peachy said, "what was it changed you? I have always wanted to ask but I have never dared. What brought you to the island finally? What made you give up the fight with us?"

The far-away look in Julia's eyes grew, if possible, more far-away. She did not speak for a while. Then, "I'll tell you," she said simply. "It is something that I have never told anybody but Billy. When you first began to leave me to come to this island alone, I was very unhappy. And I grew more and more unhappy. I missed flying with you. And especially flying by night. Flying alone seemed melancholy. I came here at first, only because I was driven by my loneliness. I said to myself that I'd drift with the current. But that did not help any. You were all so interested in your lovers that it made no difference whether I was with you or not. I began to think that you no longer cared for me, that you had outgrown me, that all my influence over you had vanished, that, if I were out of the way, the one tie which held you to me would break and you would go to these men. I grew more and more unhappy every instant. That was not all. I was in love with Billy, but I did not know it. I only knew that I was moody and strange and in desperate despair. And, so, one day I decided to kill myself."

There was a faint movement in the group, but it was only the swish of draperies as the four recumbent women came upright. They stared at Julia. They did not speak. They seemed scarcely to breathe.

"One day, I flew up and up. Never before had I gone half so high. But I flew deliberately higher and higher until I became cold and colder and numb and frozen—until my wings stopped. And then——" She paused.

"What happened?" Clara asked breathlessly.

"I dropped. I dropped like a stone. But—but—the instant I let myself go, something strange happened—a miracle of self-revelation. I knew that I loved Billy, that I could not live in any world

where he could not come to me. And the instant
that I realized that I loved him, I knew also
that I could not die. I tried to spread my
wings but they would not open. It was terrific. And that sense of despair, that my wings
which had always responded—would not—now—
oh, that was hell. How I fought! How I struggled! It was as though iron bands were about me.
I strained. I tore. Of course, all this was only
a moment. But one thinks a million things in a
moment like that—one lives a thousand years. It
seemed an eternity. At last my wings opened and
spread. They held. I floated until I caught my
breath. Then I dropped slowly. I threw myself
over the bough of a tree. I lay there."

There was an interval of intense silence.

" Did you faint? " Peachy asked in an awed
voice.

" I wept."

" You *wept*, Julia? " Peachy said. *" You! "*

" I had not wept since my childhood. It was
strange. It frightened me almost as much as the
fall. Oh, how fast the tears came—and in such

floods! Something melted and went away from me then. A softness came over me. It was like a spell. I have never been the same creature since. I cry easily now."

"Did you tell Billy?" Clara asked.

"He saw me," Julia answered.

"He saw——" It came from her four listeners as from one woman.

"That's what changed him. That's what determined him to help capture us. He said that he was afraid I would try it again. I wouldn't have, though."

Nobody spoke for a long time.

"Julia!" It was Chiquita who broke the silence this time. "There is something I, too, have always wanted to ask you. But I have never dared before. What was it tempted you to go into the Clubhouse that day? At first you tried to keep us from going in. You never seemed to care for any of the things they gave us. You threw away the fans and the slippers and the scarfs. And you smashed your mirror."

"Billy asked me this same question once," Julia

answered. "It was that big diamond—the Wilmington 'Blue.' I caught a glimpse of it through the doorway as it lay all by itself on the table, flashing in the sunlight. I had never before in my life seen any *thing* that I really wanted. But this was so exquisite, so chiseled, so tiny, so perfect, There was so much fire and color in it. It seemed like a living creature. I was enchanted by it. When I told Billy, he laughed. He said that the lust for diamonds was a recognized earth-disease among earth-people, especially earth-women. He said that many women had been ruined by it. He said that it was a common saying among men that you could catch any woman in a trap baited with diamonds. I have never got over the sting of that. I blush always when I think of it. Because—although I don't exactly understand why—it was not quite true in my case. That is a thing which always bothers me in conversation with the men. They talk about us as if they knew all about us. You'd think they'd invented us. Not that we're not simple enough. We're perfectly simple, but they've never bothered to study us. They say so many things about us, for instance, that are only half true—and yet I don't know exactly how to confute them. None of us would presume to say such things about them. I'm glad," she ended with a sudden fierceness, " that I threw the diamond away."

" Julia," and now it was Lulu who questioned, " why do you not marry Billy when you love him so?" The seriousness of her tone, the warmth of affection in her little brown face robbed this question of any appearance of impertinence.

" Lulu," Julia answered simply, " I don't know why. Only that something inside has always said, ' Wait! ' "

" Well, you did well," Peachy said bitterly, " for, at least, Billy loves you just as much as at first. I don't see him racing over to the Clubhouse the moment his dinner is eaten. I don't see him spending his Sundays in long exploring tramps. I don't see him making plans to go off into the interior for a week at a time."

" But he would be just like all the others, Julia,"

Clara exclaimed carefully, " if you'd married him. Keep out of it as long as you can!"

" Don't ever marry him, Julia," Chiquita warned. " Keep your life a perpetual wooing."

" Marry him to-morrow, Julia," Lulu advised. " Oh, I cannot think what my life would have been without Honey-Boy and Honey-Bunch."

" I shall marry Billy sometime," Julia said. " But I don't know when. When that little inner voice stops saying, ' Wait!'"

" I wonder," Peachy questioned again, " what would have happened if——"

" It would have come out just the same way. Depend on that!" Chiquita said philosophically. " It was our fate—the Great Doom that our people used to talk of. And, after all, it's our own fault. Come to this island we would and come we did! And this is the end of it—we—*we* sit moveless from sun-up to sun-down, we who have soared into the clouds. But there is a humorous element in it. And if I didn't weep, I could laugh myself mad over it. We sit here helpless and watch these creatures who *walk* desert us daily—

desert us—creatures who flew—leave us here helpless and alone."

"But in the beginning," Lulu interposed
anxiously, "they did try to take us with them.
But it tired them so to carry us—for that's what
in effect they do."

"And there was one time just after we
were married when it was all wonderful,"
said Peachy. "I did not even miss the flying,
for it seemed to me that Ralph made up for
the loss of my wings by his love and service.
Then, they began to build the New Camp
and gradually everything changed. You see,
they love their work more than they do
us. Or at least it seems to interest them
more."

"Why not?" Julia interpolated quietly. "We're
the same all the time. We don't change and grow.
Their work does change and grow. It presents new
aspects every day, new questions and problems and
difficulties, new answers and solutions and adjust-
ments. It makes them think all the time. They
love to think." She added this as one who an-

nounces a discovery, long pondered over. "They enjoy thinking."

"Yes," Lulu agreed wonderingly, "that's true, isn't it? That never occurred to me. They really do like thinking. How curious! I hate to think."

"I never think," Chiquita announced.

"I won't think," Peachy exclaimed passionately. "I *feel*. That's the way to live."

"I don't have to think," Clara declared proudly. "I've something better than thought—instinct and intuition."

Julia was silent.

"Julia is like them," Lulu said, studying Julia's absent face tenderly. "She likes to think. It doesn't hurt, or bother, or irritate, or tire—or make her look old. It's as easy for her as breathing. That's why the men like to talk to her."

"Well," Clara remarked triumphantly, "I don't have to think in order to have the men about me. I'm very glad of that."

This was true. The second year of their stay in Angel Island, the other four women had rebuked

Clara for this tendency to keep men about her—without thinking.

"It is not necessary for us to think," said Peachy with a sudden, spirited lift of her head from her shoulders. The movement brought back some of her old-time vivacity and luster. Her thick, brilliant, springy hair seemed to rise a little from her forehead. And under her draperies that which remained of what had once been wings stirred faintly. "They must think just as they must walk because they are earth-creatures. They cannot exist without infinite care and labor. We don't have to think any more than we have to walk; for we are air-creatures. And air-creatures only fly and feel. We are superior to them."

"Peachy," Julia said again. Her voice thrilled as though some thought, long held quiescent within her, had burst its way to expression. It rang like a bugle. It vibrated like a violin-string. "That is the mistake we've made all our lives; a mistake that has held us here tied to this camp for four years;—the idea that we are superior in some way, more strong, more beautiful, more good than they. But think a moment! Are we? True, we are as you say, creatures of the air. True, we were born with wings. But didn't we have to come down to the earth to eat and sleep, to love, to marry, and to bear our young? Our trouble is that——"

And just then, " Here they come!" Lulu cried happily.

Lulu's eyes turned away from the group of women. Her brown face had lighted as though somebody had placed a torch beside it. The strings of little dimples that her plumpness had brought in its wake played about her mouth.

The trail that emerged from the jungle ran between bushes, and gradually grew lower and lower, until it merged with a path shooting straight across the sand to the Playground.

For a while the heads of the file of men appeared above the bushes; then came shoulders, waists, knees; finally the entire figures. They strode through the jungle with the walk of conquerors.

They were so absorbed in talk as not to realize that the camp was in sight. Every woman's eye——

and some subtle revivifying excitement temporarily dispersed the discontent there—had found
her mate long before he remembered to look in her
direction.

The children heard the voices and immediately
raced, laughing and shouting, to meet their fa-
thers. Angela, beating her pinions in a very
frenzy of haste, arrived first. She fluttered away
from outstretched arms until she reached Ralph;
he lifted her to his breast, carried her snug-
gled there, his lips against her hair. Honey and
Pete absently swung their sons to their shoulders and went on talking. Junior, tired out by
his exertions, sat down plumply half-way. Grinning radiantly, he waited for the procession to
overtake him.

" Peachy," Julia asked in an aside, " have you
ever asked Ralph what he intends to do about
Angela's wings? "

"What he intends to do?" Peachy echoed.
"What do you mean? What can he intend to
do? What has he to say about them, anyway? "

"He may not intend anything," Julia answered gravely. "Still, if I were you, I'd have a talk with him."

Time had brought its changes to the five men as to the five women; but they were not such devastating changes.

Honey led the march, a huge wreath of uprooted blossoming plants hanging about his neck. He was at the prime of his strength, the zenith of his beauty and, in the semi-nudity that the climate permitted, more than ever like a young wood-god. Health shone from his skin in a copper-bronze that seemed to overlay the flesh like armor. Happiness shone from his eyes in a fire-play that seemed never to die down. One year more and middle age might lay its dulling finger upon him. But now he positively flared with youth.

Close behind Honey came Billy Fairfax, still shock-headed, his blond hair faded to tow, slimmer, more serious, more fine. His eyes ran ahead of the others, found Julia's face, lighted up. His gaze lingered there in a tender smile.

Just over Billy's shoulder, Pete appeared, a

Pete as thin and nervous as ever, the incipient black beard still prickling in tiny ink-spots through a skin stained a deep mahogany. There was some subtle change in Pete that was not of the flesh but of the spirit. Perhaps the look in his face—doubly wild of a Celt and of a genius—had tamed a little. But in its place had come a question: undoubtedly he had gained in spiritual dignity and in humorous quality.

Ralph Addington followed Pete. And Ralph also had changed. True, he retained his inalienable air of elegance, an elegance a little too sartorial. And even after six years of the jungle, he maintained his picturesqueness. Long-haired, liquid-eyed, still with a beard symmetrically pointed and a mustache carefully cropped, he was more than ever like a young girl's idea of an artist. And yet something different had come into his face. The slight touch of gray in his wavy hair did not account for it; nor the lines, netting delicately his long-lashed eyes. The eyes themselves bore a baffled expression, half of revolt, half of resignation; as one who has at last found the immovable obstacle, who accepts the situation even while he rebels against it.

At the end of the line came Merrill, a doubly transformed man, looking at the same time younger and handsomer. Bigger and even more muscular than formerly, his eyes were wide open and sparkling, his mouth had lost its rigidity of contour. His look of severity, of asceticism had vanished. Nothing but his classic regularity remained and that had been beautifully colored by the weather.

The five couples wound through the trail which led from the Playground to the Camp, the men half-carrying their wives with one arm about their waists and the other supporting them.

The Camp had changed. The original cabins had spread by an addition of one or two or three to sprawling bungalow size. Not an atom of their wooden structure showed. Blocks of green, cubes of color, only open doorways and windows betrayed that they were dwelling-places. A tide of tropical jungle beat in waves of green with crests of rainbow up to the very walls. There it was met by a backwash of the vines which embowered the cabins, by a stream of blossoms which flooded and cascaded down their sides.

The married ones stopped at the Camp. But Billy and Julia continued up the beach.

" How did the work go to-day, Honey? " Lulu asked in a perfunctory tone as they moved away from the Playground.

" Fine! " Honey answered enthusiastically. " You wait until you see Recreation Hall." He stopped to light his pipe. " Lord, how I wish I had some real tobacco! It's going to be a corker. We've decided to enlarge the plan by another three feet."

" Have you really? " commented Lulu. " Dear me, you've torn your shirt again."

" Yes," said Honey, puffing violently, " a nail. And we're going to have a tennis court at one side —not a little squeezed-up affair like this—but a big, fine one. We're going to lay out a golf course, too. That will be some job, Mrs. Holworthy D. Smith, and don't you forget it."

"Yes, I should think it would be," agreed Lulu. "Do you know, Honey, Clara's an awful cat! She's dreadfully jealous of Peachy. The things she says to her! She knows Pete's still half in love with her. Peachy understands him on his art side as Clara can't. Clara simply hands it to Pete if he looks at Peachy. Even when she knows that he knows, that we all know, that she tried her best to start a flirtation with you."

"And to-day," Honey interrupted eagerly, "we doped out a scheme for a series of canals to run right round the whole place—with gardens on the bank. You see we can pipe the lake water and——"

"That will be great," said Lulu, but there was no enthusiasm in her tone. "And really, Honey, Peachy's in a dreadful state of nerves. Of course, she knows that Ralph is still crazy about Julia and always will be, just because Julia's like a stone to him—oh, you know the kind of a man Ralph is. The only woman you can depend on him to be faithful to is the one that won't have him round. I don't think that bothers Peachy, though. She adores Julia. If she could fly a little while in the afternoon—an hour, say—I know it would cure her."

"Too bad. But, of course, we couldn't let you girls fly again. Besides, I doubt very much if, after so many cuttings, your wings would ever grow big enough. You don't realize it yourself, perhaps, but you're much more healthy and normal without wings."

"I don't mind being without them so much myself,"—Lulu's tone was a little doubtful—"though I think they would help me with Honey-Boy and Honey-Bunch. Sometimes——" She did not finish.

"And then," Honey went on decidedly, "it's not natural for women to fly. God never intended them to."

"It is wonderful," Lulu said admiringly, "how men know exactly what God intended."

Honey roared. "If you'd ever heard the term *sarcasm,* my dear, I should think you were slipping something over on me. In point of fact, we don't know what God intended. Nobody does. But we know better than you; the man's life broadens us."

"Then I should think——" Lulu began. But again she did not finish.

"We're going to make a tower of rocks on the central island of the lake," Honey went on. "We'll drag the stones from the beach—those big, beauty round ones. When it's finished, we're going to cover it with that vine which has the scarlet, butterfly flowers. Pete says the reflections in the water will be pretty neat."

"Really. It sounds charming. And, Honey, Chiquita is so lazy. Little Junior runs wild. He's nearly two and she hasn't made a strip of clothing for him yet. It's Frank's fault, though. He never notices anything. I really think you men ought to do something about that."

"And then," Honey went on. But he stopped. "What's the use?" he muttered under his breath. He subsided, enveloped himself in a cloud of smoke and listened, half-amused, half-irritated, to Lulu's pauseless, squirrel-like chatter.

" My dear," Frank Merrill said to Chiquita after dinner, " the New Camp is growing famously. Six months more and you will be living in your new home. The others—Pete especially—are very much interested in Recreation Hall. They have just worked out a new scheme for parks and gardens. It is very interesting, though purely decorative. It offers many absorbing problems. But, for my own part, I must confess I am more interested in the library. It will be most gratifying to see all our books ranged on shelves, classified and catalogued at last. It is a good little library as amateur libraries go. The others speak again and again of my foresight during those early months in taking care of the books. We have many fine books—what people call solid reading—and a really extraordinary collection of dictionaries. You see, many scholars travel in the Orient, and they feel they must get up on all kinds of things. I suggested to-day that we draw up a constitution for Angel Island. For by the end of twenty years, there will be a third generation growing up here. And then, the population will increase amazingly. Besides, it offers many subjects for discussion in our evenings at the Clubhouse, etc., etc., etc."

Holding the tired-out little Junior in her lap, Chiquita rocked and fanned herself and napped—and woke—and rocked and fanned herself and napped again.

" Oh, don't bore me with any talk about the New Camp," Clara was saying to Pete. " I'm not an atom interested in it."

" But you're going to live there sometime," Pete remonstrated, wrinkling in perplexity his fiery, freckled face.

" Yes, but I don't feel as if I were. It's all so far away. And I never see it. If I had anything to say about it, I might feel differently. But I haven't. So please don't inflict it on me."

" But it's the inspiration of building it for you women," Pete said gravely, " that makes us men work like slaves. We're only doing it for your sake. It is the expression of our love and admiration for you."

" Oh, slush! " exclaimed Clara flippantly, borrowing from Honey's vocabulary. " You're building it to please yourself. Besides, I don't want to be an inspiration for anything."

" All right, then," Pete said in an aggrieved tone. " But you are an inspiration, just the same. It is the chief vocation of women." He moved over to the desk and took up a bunch of papers there.

" Oh, are you going to write again this evening? " Clara asked in a burst of despair.

" Yes." Pete hesitated. " I thought I'd work for an hour or two and then I'd go out."

Clara groaned. " If you leave me another minute of this day, I shall go mad. I've had nothing but housework all the morning and then a little talk with the girls, late this afternoon. I want something different now."

" Well, let me read the third act to you," Pete offered.

" No, I don't feel like being read to. I want some excitement."

Pete sighed, and put his manuscript down.

"All right. Let's go in swimming. But I'll have to leave you after an hour."

"Are you going to see Peachy?" Clara demanded shrilly.

"No." Pete's tone was stern. "I'm going to the Clubhouse."

"How has everything gone to-day, Billy?" Julia asked, as they sat looking out to sea.

"Rather well," Billy answered. "We were all in a working mood and all in good spirits. We've done more to-day than we've done in any three days before. At noon, while we were eating our lunch, I showed them your plans."

"You didn't say——"

"I didn't peep. I promised, you know. I let them assume that they were mine. They went wild over them, threw all kinds of fits. You see, Pete has a really fine artistic sense that's going to waste in all these minor problems of construction and drainage. I flatter myself that I, too, have some taste. Addington and Honey are both good workmen—that is, they work steadily under instruction.   Merrill's only an inspired plumber, of course.   Pete and I have been feeling for a long time that we wanted to do something more creative, more esthetic.   This is just the thing we needed.   I'm glad you thought it out; for I was beginning to grow stale.   I sometimes wonder what will happen when the New Camp is entirely built and there's nothing else to do."

Billy's voice had, in spite of his temperamental optimism, a dull note of unpleasant anticipation.

" There'll be plenty to do after that."   Julia smiled reassuringly.   " I'm working on a plan to lay out the entire island.   That will take years and years and years.   Even then you'll need help."

" That, my beloved," Billy said, " until the children grow up, is just what we can't get—help."

Julia was silent.

" Julia," he went on, after an interval, in which neither spoke, " won't you marry me? I'm lonely."

The poignant look—it was almost excruciating now—came into Julia's eyes.

" Not now, Billy," she answered.

" And yet you say you love me ! '

The sadness went. Julia's face became limpid as water, bright as light, warm as flame. " I love you," she said. " I love you ! I love you ! " She went on reiterating these three words. And with every iteration, the thrill in her voice seemed to deepen. " And, Billy——"

" Yes."

" I'm not quite sure when—but I know I'm going to marry you some time."

" I'll wait, then," Billy promised. " As long as I know you love me, I can wait until—the imagination of man has not conceived the limit yet."

" Well, how have you been to-day ? " Ralph asked. But before Peachy could speak, he answered himself in a falsetto voice that parodied her round, clear accents, " I want to fly ! I want to fly ! I want to fly ! " His tone was not ill-tempered, however; and his look was humorously affectionate, as one who has asked the same question many times and received the same answer.

"I do want to fly, Ralph," Peachy said listlessly. "Won't you let me? Oh, please let my wings grow again?"

Ralph shook his head inflexibly. "Couldn't do it, my dear. It's not womanly. The air is no place for a woman. The earth is her home."

"That's not argument," Peachy asserted haughtily. "That's statement. Not that I want to argue the question. My argument is unanswerable. Why did we have wings, if not to fly. But I don't want to quarrel——" Her voice sank to pleading. "I'd always be here when you came back. You'd never see me flying. It would not prevent me from doing my duty as your wife or as Angela's mother. In fact, I could do it better because it would make me so happy and well. After a while, I could take Angela with me. Oh, that would be rapture!" Peachy's eyes gleamed.

Ralph shook his head. "Couldn't think of it, my dear. The clouds are no place for my wife. Besides, I doubt if your wings would ever grow after the clipping to which we've submitted them.

Now, put something on, and I'll carry you down on the beach."

"Tell me about the New Camp, and what you did to-day!" Peachy asked, after an interval in which she visibly struggled for control.

"Oh, Lord, ask anything but that," Addington exclaimed with a sudden gust of his old irritability. "I work hard enough all day. When I get home, I want to talk about something else. It rests me not to think of it."

"But, Ralph," Peachy entreated, "I could help you. I know I could. I have so many ideas about things. You know Pete says I'm a real artist. It would interest me so much if you would only talk over the building plans with me."

"I don't know that I am particularly interested in Pete's opinion of your abilities," Addington rejoined coldly. "My dear little girl," he went on, palpably striving for patience and gentleness, "there's nothing you could do to help me. Women are too impractical. This is a man's work, besides. By the way, after we've had our little outing, I'll leave you with Lulu. Honey and Pete and I are going to meet at the Clubhouse to work over some plans."

"All right," Peachy said. She added, "I guess I won't go out, after all. I feel tired. I think I'll lie down for a while."

"Anything I can do for you, dear?" Addington asked tenderly as he left.

"Nothing, thank you." Peachy's voice was stony. Then suddenly she pulled herself upright on the couch. "Oh—Ralph—one minute. I want to talk to you about Angela. Her wings are growing so fast."

VII

"WHERE'S Peachy?" Julia asked casually the next afternoon.

"I've been wondering where she was, too," Lulu answered. "I think she must have slept late this morning. I haven't seen her all day."

"Is Angela with the children now?" Julia went on.

"I suppose so," Lulu replied. She lifted herself from the couch. Shading her hands, she studied the group at the water's edge. Honey-Boy and Peterkin were digging wells in the sand. Junior making futile imitative movements, followed close at their heels. Near the group of women, Honey-Bunch crept across the mat of pine-needles, chasing an elusive sunbeam. "No, she's not there."

"Now that I think of it, Angela didn't come to play with Peterkin this morning," said Clara.

"Generally she comes flying over just after breakfast."

"You don't suppose Peachy's ill," asked Chiquita, "or Angela."

"Oh, no!" Lulu answered. "Ralph would have told one of us."

"Here she comes up the trail now," Chiquita exclaimed. "Angela's with her."

"Yes—but what's the matter?" Lulu cried. "She's all bent over and she's staggering."

"She's crying," said Clara, after a long, intent look.

"Yes," said Lulu. "She's crying hard. And look at Angela—the darling! She's trying to comfort her."

Peachy was coming slowly towards them; slowly because, although both hands were on the rail, she staggered and stumbled. At intervals, she dropped and crawled on hands and knees. At intervals, convulsions of sobbing shook her, but it was voiceless sobbing. And those silent cataclysms, taken with her blind groping progress, had a sinister quality. Lulu and Julia tottered to meet her. " What is it, oh, what is it, Peachy? " they cried.

Peachy did not reply immediately. She fought to control herself. " Go down to the beach, baby," she said firmly to Angela. " Stay there until mother calls you. Fly away! "

The little girl fluttered irresolutely. " Fly away, dear! " Peachy repeated. Angela mounted a breeze and made off, whirling, circling, dipping, and soaring, in the direction of the water. Once or twice, she paused, dropped and, bounding from earth to air, turned her frightened eyes back to her mother's face. But each time, Peachy waved her on. Angela joined Honey-Boy and Peterkin. For a moment she poised in the air; then she sank and began languidly to dig in the sand.

" I couldn't let her hear it," Peachy said. " It's about her. Ralph——" She lost control of herself for a moment; and now her sobs had voice. " I asked him last night about Angela and her flying. I don't exactly know why I did. It was something you said to me yesterday, Julia, that put it into my head. He said that when she was eighteen, he was going to cut her wings just as he cut mine."

There came clamor from her listeners. "Cut Angela's wings!" "Why?" "What for?"

Peachy shook her head. "I don't know yet why, although he tried all night, to make me understand. He said that he was going to cut them for the same reason that he cut mine. He said that it was all right for her to fly now when she was a baby and later when she was a very young girl, that it was 'girlish' and 'beautiful' and 'lovely' and 'charming' and 'fascinating' and— and—a lot of things. He said that he could not possibly let her fly when she became a woman, that then it would be 'unwomanly' and 'unlovely' and 'uncharming' and 'unfascinating.' He said that even if he were weak enough to allow it, her husband never would. I could not understand his argument. I could *not*. It was as if we were talking two languages. Besides, I could scarcely talk, I cried so. I've cried for hours and hours and hours."

"Sit down, Peachy," Julia advised gently.

"Let us all sit down." The women sank to their couches. But they did not lounge; they continued to sit rigidly upright. "What are you going to do, Peachy?"

"I don't know. But I'll throw myself into the ocean with Angela in my arms before I'll consent to have her wings cut. Why, the things he said. Lulu, he said that Angela might marry Honey-Boy, as they were the nearest of age. He said that Honey-Boy would certainly cut her wings, that he, no more than Honey, could endure a wife who flew. He said that all earth-men were like that. Lulu, would you let your child do—do—that to my child?"

Lulu's face had changed—almost horribly. Her eyes glittered between narrowed lids. Her lips had pulled away from each other, baring her teeth. "You tell Ralph he's mistaken about my son," she ground out.

"That's what I told him," Peachy went on in a breaking voice. "But he said you wouldn't have anything to do or say about it. He said that Honey-Boy would be trained in these matters by his father, not by his mother. I said that you would fight them both. He asked me what chance you would have against your husband and your son. He—he—he always spoke as if Honey-Boy were more Honey's child than yours, and as though Angela were more his child than mine. He said that he had talked this question over with the other men when Angela's wings first began to grow. He said that they made up their minds then that her wings must be cut when she became a woman. I besought him not to do it—I begged, I entreated, I pleaded. He said that nothing I could say would change him. I said that you would all stand by me in this, and he asked me what we five could do against them. He called us five tottering females. Oh, it grew dreadful. I shrieked at him, finally. As he left, he said, ' Remember your first day in the Clubhouse, my dear! That's my answer.' " She turned to Clara. " Clara, you are going to bear a child in the spring. It may be a girl. Would you let son of mine or any of these women clip her wings? Will you suffer Peterkin to clip Angela's wings? "

Clara's whole aspect had fired. Flame seemed to burst from her gray-green eyes, sparks to shoot from her tawny head. " I would strike him dead first."

Peachy turned to Chiquita. The color had poured into Chiquita's face until her full brown eyes glared from a purple mask. " You, too, Chiquita. You may bear girl-children. Oh, will you help me? "

" I'll help you," Chiquita said steadily. She added after a pause, " I cannot believe that they'll dare, though."

" Oh, they'll dare anything," Peachy said bitterly. " Earth-men are devils. What shall we do, Julia? " she asked wearily.

Julia had arisen. She stood upright. Curiously, she did not totter. And despite her shorn pinions, she seemed more than ever to tower like some Winged Victory of the air. Her face glowed with rage. As on that fateful day at the Clubhouse, it was as though a fire had been built in an alabaster vase. But as they looked at her, a rush of tears wiped the flame from her eyes. She sank back again on the couch. She put her hands over her face and sobbed. "At last," she said strangely. "At last! At last! At last!"

"What shall we do, Julia?" Peachy asked stonily.

"Rebel!" answered Julia.

"But how?"

"Refuse to let them cut Angela's wings."

"Oh, I would not dare open the subject with Ralph," Peachy said in a terror-stricken voice. "In the mood he's in, he'd cut her wings to-night."

"I don't mean to tell him anything about it," Julia replied. "Rebel in secret. I mean—they overcame us once by strategy. We must beat them now by superior strategy."

"You don't really mean anything secret, do you, Julia?" Lulu remonstrated. "That wouldn't be quite fair, would it?"

And curiously enough, Julia answered in the exact words that Honey had used once. "Anything's fair in love or war—and this is both. We can't be fair. We can't trust them. We trusted them once. Once is enough for me."

"But how, Julia?" Peachy asked. Her voice had now a note of querulousness in it. "How are we going to rebel?"

Julia started to speak. Then she paused. "There's something I must ask you first. Tell me, all of you, what did you do with your wings when the men cut them off?"

The rage faded out of the four faces. A strange reticence seemed to blot out expression. The reticence changed to reminiscence, to a deep sadness.

Lulu spoke first. "I thought I was going to keep my wings as long as I lived. I always thought of them as something wonderful, left over from a happier time. I put them away, done up in silk. And at first I used to look at them every day. But I was always sad afterwards—and—and gradually, I stopped doing it. Honey hates to come home and find me sad. Months went by—I only looked at them occasionally. And after a while, I did not look at them at all. Then, one day, after Honey built the fireplace for me, I saw that we needed something—to—to—to sweep the hearth with. I tried all kinds of things, but nothing was right. Then, suddenly, I remembered my wings. It had been two years since I'd looked at them. And after that long time, I found that I didn't care so much. And so—and so—one day I got them out and cut them into little brooms for the hearth. Honey never said anything about it—but I knew he knew. Somehow——" A strange expression came into the face of the unanalytic Lulu. "I always have a feeling that Honey enjoys using my wings about the hearth."

Julia hesitated. "What did you do, Chiquita?"

"Oh, I had all Lulu's feeling at first, of course. But it died as hers did. You see this fan. You have often commented on how well I've kept it all these years—I've mended it from month to month with feathers from my own wings. The color is becoming to me—and Frank likes me to carry a fan. He says that it makes him think of a country called Spain that he always wanted to visit when he was a youth."

"And you, Clara?" Julia asked gently.

"Oh, I went through," Clara replied, "just what Lulu and Chiquita did. Then, one day, I said to myself, 'What's the use of weeping over a dead thing?' I made my wings into wall-decorations. You're right about Honey, Lulu." For a moment there was a shade of conscious coquetry in Clara's voice. "I know that it gives Pete a feeling of satisfaction—I don't exactly know why (unless it's a sense of having conquered)—to see my wings tacked up on his bedroom walls."

Peachy did not wait for Julia to put the question to her. "As soon as I could move, after they freed us from the Clubhouse, I threw mine into the sea. I knew I should go mad if I kept them where I could see them every day. Just to look at them was like a sharp knife going through my heart. One night, while Ralph was asleep, I crawled out of the house on my hands and knees, dragging them after me. I crept down to the beach and threw them into the water. They did not sink—they floated. I stayed until they drifted out of sight. The moon was up. It shone on them. Oh, the glorious blue of them—and the glitter—the—the——" But Peachy could not go on.

"What did you do with yours, Julia?" Lulu asked at last.

"I kept them until last night," Julia answered. "Among the ship's stuff was a beautiful carved chest. It was packed with linen. Billy said it was some earth-girl's wedding outfit. I took everything out of the chest and put my wings in it. Folded carefully, they just fitted. I used to brood over them every night before I went to bed. Oh, they were wonderful in the dark—as if the chest were full of white fire. Many times I've waked up in the middle of the night and gone to look at them. I don't know why, but I had to do it. After a while, it hurt me so much that I made up my mind to lock the chest forever; for I always wept. I could not help it."

Julia wept now. The tears poured down her cheeks. But she went on.

"After yesterday's talk, I thought this situation over for a long time. Then I went to the chest,

took out my wings, brought them downstairs and
—and—and——"

"What?" somebody whispered.

"Burned them!" Julia's deep voice swelled
on the word "burned" as though she still felt
the scorching agony of that moment.

For a long moment, nobody spoke.

Julia asked their question for them. "Do you
want to know why I did it?" And without waiting, she answered, "Because I wanted to mark in
some way the end of my desire to fly. We must
stop wanting to fly, we women. We must stop
wasting our energy brooding over what's past.
We must stop it at once. Not only that but—for
Angela's sake and for the sake of all girl-children
who will be born on this island—we must learn
to walk."

"Learn to walk!" Peachy repeated. "Julia,
have you gone mad? We have always held out
against this degradation. We must continue to
do so." Again came that proud lift of her shoulders, the vibrant stir of wing-stumps. "That
would lower us to a level with men."

" But are we lowering ourselves? " Julia asked. " Are they really on a lower level? Isn't the earth as good as the air? "

" It's better, Julia," Lulu said unexpectedly. " The earth's a fine place. It's warm and home-like. Things grow there. There's nothing in the air."

" There are the stars," murmured Peachy.

" Yes," said Julia with a soft tenderness, " but we never reached them."

" The air-life may not have been better or finer," Peachy continued, " but, somehow, it seemed clearer and purer. The earth's such a cluttered place. It's so full of *things*. You can hardly see it for the stuff that's on it. From above it seems beautiful, but near——"

" Yet, it is on the earth that we must live— and that Angela must live," Julia interpolated gently.

" But what is the use of our learning to walk? " Peachy demanded.

" To teach Angela how to walk and all the other girl-children that are coming to us."

"But I am afraid," Peachy said anxiously, "that if Angela learned to walk, she would forget how to fly."

"On the contrary," Julia declared, "she would fly better for knowing how to walk, and walk better for knowing how to fly."

"I don't see it," interposed Clara emphatically. "I don't see what we get out of walking or what Angela will get out of it. Suppose we learned to walk? The men would stop helping us along. We'd lose the appeal of helplessness."

"But what is there about what you call 'the appeal of helplessness' that makes it worth keeping?" Julia asked, smiling affectionately into Clara's eyes. "Why shouldn't we lose it?"

"Why, because," Clara exclaimed indignantly, "because—because—why, because," she ended lamely. Then, with one of her unexpected bursts of mental candor, "I'm sure I don't know why," she admitted, "except that we have always appealed to them for that reason. Then again," she took up her argument from another angle, "if we learn to walk, they won't wait on us any more.

They may even stop giving us things. As it is now, they're really very generous to us."

The others smiled with varying degrees of furtiveness. Pete, as they all knew, could always placate an incensed Clara by offering her some loot of the homeward way: a bunch of flowers, a handful of nuts, beautifully colored pebbles, shells with the iridescence still wet on them. She soon tired of these toys, but she liked the excitement of the surprise.

"Generous to us!" Chiquita burst out—and this was as unexpected as Lulu's face-about. "Well, when you come to that, they're never generous to us. They make us pay for all they give us. They seem generous—but they aren't really—any more than we are."

"They are far from generous," said Peachy. "They are ungenerous. They're tyrants. They're despots. See how they took advantage of our innocence and ignorance of earth-conditions."

"I protest." A note that they had never heard from Julia made steel of the thrilling melody of her voice. "You must know that is **not** true!" she said in an accusing voice. "Be fair to them! Tell the truth to yourselves! If they took advantage of our innocence and ignorance, it was we who tempted them to it in the first place. As for our innocence and ignorance—you speak as if they were beautiful or desirable. We were innocent and ignorant of earth-conditions because we were too proud to learn about them, because we always assumed that we lowered ourselves by knowing anything about them. Our mistake was that we learned to fly before we learned to walk."

"But, Julia, what are we going to do about Angela?" Peachy asked impatiently.

"I'm coming to that presently," Julia answered. "But before—I want to ask you a question. Do you remember the big cave in the northern reef— the one we used to hide in?"

"Oh, I remember," Lulu said, "perfectly."

"Did you ever tell Honey about it?" Julia turned to her directly.

"No. Why, we promised never to tell, didn't we? In case we ever needed a place of refuge——"

"Have any of you ever told about it?" Julia turned to the others. "Think carefully! This is important."

"I never have told," Peachy said wearily. "But about Angela——"

"Have you, Chiquita?" Julia interrupted with a strange insistence.

"I have never thought of it from that day to this," Chiquita answered.

"Nor I," replied Clara. "I'm not sure that I could go to it now. Could you, Julia?"

"Oh, yes," Julia answered eagerly, "I've——" She stopped abruptly. "But now I want to talk to you, and I want you to listen carefully. I am going to tell you why I think we should learn to walk. It is, in brief, for Angela's sake and for the sake of every girl-child that is born on this island. For a long time, you will think that I am talking about other things. But you must be patient. I have seen this situation coming ever since Angela's wings began to grow. I could not hurry it—but I knew it must come. Many nights I have lain awake, planning what I should say to

you when the time came. The time has come—and
I am going to say it. It is a long, long speech that
I shall deliver; and I am going to speak very
plainly. But you must not get angry—for you
know how much I love you and how much I love
your children.

" I'm going back to our young girlhood, to the
time when our people were debating the Great
Flight. We thought that we were different from
them all, we five, that we were more original and
able and courageous. And we *were* different. For
when our people decided to go south to the Snow-
lands, the courage of rebellion grew in us and we
deserted in the night. Do you remember the wonderful sense of freedom that came to us, and how
the further north we flew, the stronger it became?
When we found these islands, it seemed to us that
they must have been created especially for us.
Here, we said, we would live always, free from
earth-ties—five incorruptible air-women.

" Then the men came. I won't go into all that.
We've gone over it hundreds and hundreds of
times, just as we did this afternoon, playing the

most pathetic game we know—the do-you-remember game. But after they came, we found that we were not free from earth-ties. For the Great Doom overtook us and we fell in love. Then came the capture. And we lost our wings."

She paused a moment.

"Do you remember that awful day at the Club-house, how Chiquita comforted us? I—I failed you then; I fainted; I felt myself to blame for your betrayal. But Chiquita kept saying, 'Don't be afraid. They won't hurt us. We are precious to them. They would rather die than lose us. They need us more than we need them. They are bound to us by a chain that they cannot break.' And for a long time that seemed true. What we had to learn was that we needed them just as much as they needed us, that we were bound to them by a chain that *we* could not break.

"I often think "—Julia's voice had become dreamy—"now when it is so different, of those first few months after the capture. How kind they were to us, how gentle, how considerate, how delicate, how chivalrous! Do you remember that they treated us as if we were children, how, for a long time, they pretended to believe in fairies? Do you remember the long fairy-hunts in the moonlit jungle, the long mermaid-hunts in the moonlit ocean? Do you remember the fairy-tales by the fire? It seemed to me then that life was one long fairy-tale. And how quickly we learned their language! Has it ever occurred to you that no one of them has ever bothered to learn ours—none except Frank, and he only because he was mentally curious? Then came the long wooing. How we argued the marriage question—discussed and debated—each knowing that the Great Doom was on her and could not be gainsaid.

"Then came the betrothal, the marriages, and suddenly all that wonderful starlight and firelight life ended. For a while, the men seemed to drift away from each other. For a while, we—the 'devoted five,' as our people called us—seemed to drift away from each other. It was as though they took back something they had freely given each other to give to us. It was as though we took back something we had freely given each other to give to them.

"Then, just as suddenly, they began to drift away from us and back to each other. Some of the high, worshiping quality in their attitude toward us disappeared. It was as though we had become less beautiful, less interesting, less desirable—as if possession had killed some precious, perishable quality.

"What that quality is I do not know. We are not dumb like stones or plants, we women. We are not dull like birds or beasts. We do not fade in a day like flowers. We do not stop like music. We do not go out like light. What it was that went, or when or how, I do not know. But it was something that thrilled and enchanted them. It went—and it went forever.

"It was as though we were toys—new toys—with a secret spring. And if one found and pressed that spring, something unexpected and something unbelievably wonderful would happen. They hunted for that spring untiringly—hunted—

and hunted—and hunted.   At last they found it.
And after they found it, we no longer interested
them.   The mystery and fascination had gone.
After all, a toy is only a toy.

"Then came our great trouble—that terrible
time of the illicit hunting.   Every man of them
making love to some one of you.   Every woman
of you making love to some one of them.   That
was a year of despair for me.   I could see no way
out.   It seemed to me that you were all drifting
to destruction and that I could not stay you.
And then I began to realize that the root of evil
was only one thing—idleness.   Idle men!   Idle
women!   And as I wondered what we should do
next, Nature took the matter in her hands.   She
gave all you women work to do."

Julia paused.   Her still gray eyes fixed on far-
away things.

"Honey-Boy was born, then Peterkin, then
Angela, then Honey-Bunch.   And suddenly everything was right again.   But, somehow, the men
seemed soon to exhaust the mystery and fascination of fatherhood just as they had exhausted the

mystery and fascination of husbandhood. They became restless and irritable. It seemed to me that another danger beset us—vague, monstrous, looming—but I did not know what. You see they have the souls of discoverers and explorers and conquerors, these earth-men. They are creators. Their souls are filled with an eternal unrest. Always they must attempt one thing more; ever they seek something beyond. They would stop the sun and the moon in their courses; they would harness the hurricane; they would chain the everlasting stars. Sea, earth, sky are but their playgrounds; past, present, future their servants; they lust to conquer the unexplored areas of space and time. It came to me that what they needed was work of another kind. One night, when I was lying awake thinking it over, the idea of the New Camp burst on my mind. Do you remember how delighted they were when I suggested it to them, how delighted you were, how gay and jubilant we all were, how, for days and days, we talked of nothing else? And we were as happy over the idea as they. For a long time, we thought that we were going to help.

"We thought that we were going with them every day, not to work but to sit in the nearby shade, to encourage them with our praise and appreciation. And we did go for a month. But they had to carry us all the way—or nearly carry us. Think of that—supporting a full-grown woman all that weary road. I saw the feeling begin to grow in them that we were burdens. I watched it develop. Understand me, a beautiful burden, a beloved burden, but still a burden, a burden that it would be good to slip off the back for the hours of the working day. I could not blame them. For we were burdens. Then, under one pretext or another, they began to suggest to us not to go daily to the New Camp with them. The sun was too hot; we might fall; insects would sting us; the sudden showers were too violent. Finally, that if we did not watch the New Camp grow, it would be a glorious surprise to us when it was finished.

"At first, you were all touched and delighted with their gallantry—but I—I knew what it meant.

" I tried to stem the torrent of their strange absorption, but I could not. It grew and grew. And now you see what has happened. It has been months since one of us has been to the New Camp and all of you, except Peachy and myself, have entirely lost interest in it. It is not surprising. It is natural. I, too, would lose interest if I did not force myself to talk with Billy about it every night of my life. Lulu said yesterday that it seemed strange to her that, after working together all day, they should want to get together in the Clubhouse at night. For a long time that seemed strange to me—until I discovered that there is a chain binding them to each other even as there is a chain binding them to us. And the Bond of Work is stronger than the Bond of Sex because Work is a living, growing thing.

" In the meantime, we have our work too—the five children. But it is a little constructive work— not a great one. For in this beautiful, safe island, there is not much that we can do besides feed them. And so, here we sit day after day, five women who could once fly, big, strong, full-bodied,

teeming with various efficiencies and abilities—
wasted. If we had kept our wings, we could have
been of incalculable assistance to them. Or if we
could walk——

"But I won't go further into *our* situation. I
want to consider Angela's.

"You are wondering what all this has to do
with the matter of Angela's flying. And now I am
going to tell you. Don't you see if they wait until
she is a woman before they cut her wings, she will
be in the same case that we are in, unable either
to fly or to walk. Rather would I myself cut her
wings to-night and force her to walk. But on the
other hand, should she grow to womanhood with
wings, she would be no true mate to a wingless
man unless she could also walk. No, we must see
to it that she both flies and walks. In that case,
she will be a perfect mate to the wingless man.
Her strength will not be as great as his—but her
facility will be greater. She will walk well enough
to keep by his side; and her flying will supplement
his powers.

"And then—oh, don't you see it—don't you see

why we must fight—fight—fight for Angela, don't
you see why her wings are a sacred trust with us?
Sometime, there will be born here—— Clara,"
she turned her look on Clara's excited face, " it
may be the baby that's coming to you in the spring
—sometime there will be born here a boy with
wings. Then more and more often they will come
until there are as many winged men as winged
women. What will become of our girl-children
then if their mates fly as well as walk away from
them. There is only one way out. And there is
only one duty before us—to learn to walk that
we may teach our daughters to walk—to preserve
our daughter's wings that they may teach their
sons to fly."

" But, Julia," Peachy exclaimed, after an instant
of dead silence. There was a stir of wonder,
flute-like in her voice, a ripple of wonder, flame-
like on her face. " Our feet are too fine, too soft.
Ralph says that mine are only toy feet, that no
creature could really get along on them."

She kicked the loose sandals off. Tiny, slim,
delicately chiseled, her feet were of a china white-

ness, except where, at the tips, the toes showed a rose-flush or where, over the instep, the veins meandered in a blue network.

"Of course Peachy's feet are smaller than mine," Lulu said wistfully. "But even my workaday little pads wouldn't carry me many steps." From under her skirts appeared a pair of capable-looking, brown feet, square, broad but little and satin-smooth.

"Mine are quite useless," Chiquita sighed. "Oh, why did I let myself grow so big?" There was a note of despair in her velvet voice. "It's almost as if there were no muscles in them." She pulled aside her scarlet draperies. In spite of her increasing size, her dusky feet had kept their aristocratic Andalusian lines.

"And I've always done just the things that would make it impossible for me to walk," said Clara in a discouraged tone. "I've always taken as much care of my feet as my hands—they're like glass." This was true. In the pale-gold of her skin, the pink nails glittered brilliantly.

"And think of your own feet, Julia," Lulu

exclaimed. "They're like alabaster. Pete says that from the artist's point of view, they're absolutely perfect. You don't imagine for an instant that you could take a step on them, unsupported?"

"No?" said Julia. "No?" With a swift leap of her body, she stood on the feet in question. And as the other stared, stupefied, she walked with the splendid, swinging gait of an Amazon once, twice, thrice around the Playground.

"Come, Angela!" Peachy called. "Come, baby!"

Angela started to spread her pinions. "Don't fly, baby," Peachy called. "Walk!"

Obediently, Angela dropped her wings, sank. Her feet, shell-like, pinky-soft, padded the ground. She tried to balance, but she swayed and fell.

"No matter, darling!" Peachy called cheerily. "Try again!"

Angela heroically pulled herself up. She made

a few uncertain steps, but she stumbled with every move.

Honey-Boy and Peterkin came running up to her side; Junior, grinning happily, waddled behind a long way in the rear. " Angela's trying to walk! " the boys cried. " Angela's trying to walk! " They capered with amusement. " Oh, isn't she funny? Look at the girl trying to walk! "

The tears spurted from Angela's eyes. Her lips quivered. Her wings shot up straight.

" Don't mind what the boys say, Angela! " Peachy called. " Put your wings down! Keep right on walking! "

Again Angela's pinions dropped. Again she took a few steps. This time she fell to her knees. But she pulled herself up, sped onward, fell again, and again. She had reached the stones that bounded the sand. When she arose this last time, her foot was bleeding.

" Keep on walking, baby! " Peachy commanded inflexibly. But there was a rain of tears on her cheek.

Angela staggered forward a rod or two; and

now both feet left a trail of blood. Then suddenly again she struggled for balance, fell headlong.

"Keep on walking, mother's heart's treasure," Peachy commanded. She dropped to her knees and held out her arms; her face worked uncontrollably.

Angela pulled herself up with a determined settling of her little rose-petal mouth. Swaying, stumbling, staggering, she ran on in one final spurt until she collapsed in her mother's arms.

VIII

AND as soon as we finish the New Camp,"
Honey said eagerly, " we must make another on the rocks at the north. That will be
our summer place."

" And as soon as we've finished that, let's build
a house-boat for the lake," Billy suggested.

" Then let's put up some hunting-boxes at the
south," Ralph took it up.

" There's a good year's work on the New
Camp," Frank reminded them.

" But after the New Camp and the Hunting-
Boxes and the House-Boat—what? " Ralph asked
a little drearily.

" Plenty to do," Billy promised cheerily. " I've
been working on a plan to lay out the entire island
in camps and parks. Pete, I want to bring them
over to you some night."

" Come to-night," Pete said eagerly.

"Why not bring them to the Clubhouse," Honey asked. "I'd like to see them, too. While I'm working with my hands on one job, I like to be working with my head on the next."

"Sure," agreed Ralph, "I'm for that. I'll join you to-night. Can you come, Frank?"

"I had meant to write to-night," Frank said. "But of course I can put that off."

"Has it ever occurred to you fellows," Billy asked, "that just as soon as the boys are big enough for us to leave the women in their care, we can build a boat and visit the other four islands?"

"Gee!" Honey said. "Now you're shouting. I never thought of that. Lord, how I would like to get away from this place for a while. Being shut in in any way always gets on my nerves."

Ralph drew a long breath. "I never thought of it," he admitted. "But it gives me a new lease of life."

"I shall feel like Columbus," Pete acknowledged, "and then some. Why it's like visiting the moon—or Mars. And God knows we'll need an-

other island or two in our business—provided we
stay here for two or three generations more.
We'll be a densely populated world-center before
we know it."

"I was thinking," Billy suddenly relapsed to
the previous subject. "How about the women to-
night? They always hate to have us leave them
when we've been away all day,—and we've been
here two days, remember."

"Oh, that's all right," Honey answered.
"I'm sure Lulu'll be all right. There's been the
greatest change in her in the last few months."

"Peachy won't mind," said Ralph. "She told
me the other night to go to the Clubhouse as often
as I wanted and stay as late."

"Clara says practically the same." Pete wrin-
kled his forehead in perplexity. "It took my
breath away. How do you account for it?"

"Oh, that's all right," Honey answered.
stopping to dash the sweat from his forehead, "I
should say it was just a matter of their getting
over their foolishness. I suppose all young married women have it—that instinct to monopolize

their husbands. And when you think it over, we do sort of give them the impression while we're courting them that they are the whole cheese. But that isn't all. They've come to their senses on some other matters. I think, for instance, they're beginning to get our point of view on this flying proposition. Lulu hasn't hinted that she'd like to fly for three months. She's never been so contented since we captured them. To do her justice, though, she always saw, when I pointed it out to her, that flying was foolish, besides being dangerous."

"Well," Ralph said, "what between holding them down from the clouds and keeping them away from the New Camp, managing them has been some job. But I guess you're right, Honey. I think they're reconciled now to their lot. If I do say it as shouldn't, Peachy seems like a regular woman nowadays. She's braced up in fine style in the last two months. Her color is much better; her spirits are high. When I get home at night, she doesn't want to go out at all. If I say that I'm going to the Clubhouse, she never raises a yip. In fact, she seems too tired to care. She's always ready now to turn in when I do. For months and months, you know, she sat up reading until all hours of the night and morning. But now she falls asleep like a child."

"Then she's gotten over that insomnia?" Pete asked this casually and he did not look at Ralph.

"Entirely," Ralph replied briefly, and in his turn he did not look at Pete. "She's a perfectly healthy woman now. She gets her three squares every day and her twelve hours every night— regular. I never saw such an improvement in a woman."

"Well, when it comes to sleeping," Pete said, "I don't believe she's got anything on Clara. I often find her dead to the world when I get home at night. I jolly her about that—for she has always thought going to bed early indicated lack of temperament. And as for teasing to be allowed to fly, or to be taken out swimming, or to call on any of you, or to let her tag me here— why, that's all stopped short. She keeps dozing off all the evening. Sometimes in the midst of a

sentence, she'll begin to nod. Never saw her looking so well, though."

"Chiquita, on the contrary, isn't sleeping as
much as she did," Frank said. "She's more
active, though—physically, I mean. She's rejoic-
ing at present over the fact that she's lost twenty-
five pounds in the last three months. She said last
night that she hadn't been so slim since she was
a girl."

"Twenty-five pounds!" exclaimed Honey.
"That's a good deal to lose. How the hell—how
do you explain it!"

"Increased household activity," Frank replied
vaguely. "And then mentally, I think she's more
vigorous. She's been reading a great deal by herself. Formerly I found that reading annoyed her
—even when I read aloud, explaining carefully as
I went along."

"I haven't noticed an increased activity on
Julia's part," Billy said thoughtfully. "But she's
always been extraordinarily active, considering
everything. The way she gets about is marvelous. But of course she's planned the placing

of her furniture with that in view. She's as quick
as a cat. I have noticed, however, that she seems
much happier. They certainly are a changed lot
of women."

"The twelve o'clock whistle has just blown,"
Honey announced. "Let's eat."

The five men dropped their tools. They gathered their lunches together and fell to a voracious
feeding. At last, pipes appeared. They stretched
themselves to the smoker's ease. For a while, the
silence was unbroken. Then, here and there, somebody dropped an irrelevant remark. Nobody answered it.

They lay in one corner of the big space which
had been cleared from the jungle chaos. On one
side rippled the blue lake curving into many tiny
bays and inlets and padded with great green
oases of matted lily-leaves. On the other side
rose the highest hill on the island. The cleared
land stretched to the very summit of this hill.
Over it lay another chaos, the chaos of confusion; half-completed buildings of log and stone,
rectangles and squares of dug-up land where build-

ings would some day stand, half-finished roadways, ditches of muddy water, hills of round beach-stones, piles of logs, some stripped of the bark, others still trailing a green huddle of leaf and branch, tools everywhere. The jungle rolled like a tidal wave to the very boundary; in places its green spume had fallen over the border. As the men smoked, their eyes went back to the New Camp again and again. It was obvious that constantly they made mental measurements, that ever in their mind's eye they saw the completed thing.

"Well," said Ralph, reverting without warning to the subject under discussion. His manner tacitly assumed that the others had also been considering it mentally. "I confess I don't understand women really. I've always thought that I did. But I see now that I never have." Addington's rare outbursts of frankness in regard to the other sex were the more startling because they contrasted so sharply with his normal attitude of lordly understanding and contempt. "I've been a good manager and I'm not saying that I haven't had my successes with them. But as I look back upon them now, I realize I followed my intuitions, not my reason. I've done what I've done without knowing why. I have to feel my way still. I can't account for the change that's come over them. For four years now they've been at us to let their wings grow again. And for four years we've been saying *no* in every possible tone of voice and with every possible inflection. I've had no idea that Peachy would ever get over it. My God, you fellows have no idea what I've been through with her in regard to this question of flying. Why, one night three months ago, she had an awful attack of hysteria because I told her I'd have to cut Angela's wings as soon as she was grown-up."

" Well, what did she expect? " Honey asked.

" That I'd let her keep them—that I'd let her fly the way Peachy did! Or—what do you suppose she suggested?—that I cut them off now."

" Well, what was her idea in that? " Billy's tone was the acme of perplexity.

" That as long as I wouldn't let her keep them after she had attained her growth, she might as well not have them at all."

Billy laughed. " That's a woman's reasoning all right, all right. Why, it would destroy half Angela's charm in my eyes. That little fluttering flight of hers, half on the ground, half in the air, is so lovely, so engaging, so endearing—— But of course letting her fly high would be——"

" Absurd," Ralph interrupted.

" Dangerous," Honey interpolated.

" Unwomanly," Pete added.

" Immodest," Billy concluded.

" Well, thank God it's all over," Ralph went on. " But, as I say, I give up guessing what's changed her, unless it's the principle that constant dropping wears away the stone. Oscar Wilde had the answer. They're sphinxes without secrets. They do anything that occurs to them and for no particular reason. I get along with them only by laying down the law and holding them to it. And I reckon they've got that idea firmly fixed in their minds now—that they're to stay where we put them."

Honey wriggled as if in discomfort. " Seems to me, Ralph, you take a pretty cold-blooded view of the situation. I guess I don't go very far with you. Not that I pretend to understand women. I don't. My system with them is to give them anything they ask, within reason, of course, to keep them busy and happy, buy them presents, soft-soap them, jolly them along. I suppose that personally, I wouldn't have minded their flying a little every afternoon, as long as they took the proper care. I mean by that, not to fly too far out to sea or too high in the air and never when we were at home, so long, in short, as they followed the rules that we laid down for them. You fellows seem to have the idea if we let them do that we'd lose them. But if there's one general proposition fixed more firmly in my nut than any other, it is that you can't lose them. But of course I intend always to stand by whatever you-all say."

" I don't know," Billy burst in hotly, " which of you two makes me sickest and which is the most insulting in his attitude towards women, you, Ralph, who treat them as if they were household pets, or you, Honey, who treat them as if they were dolls. In my opinion there is only one law to govern a man's relation with a woman—the law of chivalry. To love her, and cherish her, to do all the hard work of the world for her, to stand between her and everything that is unbeautiful and unpleasant, to think for her, to put her on a pedestal and worship her; to my mind that sums up the whole duty of man to woman."

"They're better than goddesses on pedestals," Pete said. " They're creatures neither of flesh nor of marble—they're ideals. They're made of stars, sunlight, moonshine. I believe in treating them like beings of a higher world."

"I disagree with all of you," Frank said ponderously, "I don't believe in treating them as if they were pets or dolls, or goddesses on pedestals or ideals. I believe in treating them like human beings, the other half of the race. I don't see that they are any better or any worse than we— they're about the same. Soon after we captured them, you remember, we entered into an agreement that no one of us would ever let his wife's wings grow without the consent of all the others.

One minute after I had given my word, I was sorry for it. But you kept your word to me in the agreement that I forced on you before the capture; and, so, I shall always keep mine to you. But I regret it more and more as time goes on. You see I'm so constituted that I can't see anything but abstract justice. And according to abstract justice we have no right to hold these women bound to the earth. If the air is their natural habitat, it is criminal for us to keep them out of it. They're our equals in every sense—I mean in that they supplement us, as we supplement them. They've got what we haven't got and we've got what they haven't got. They can't walk, but they can fly. We can't fly, but we can walk. It is as though they compelled us, creatures of the earth, to live in the air all the time. Oh, it's wrong. You'll see it some day."

"I never listened to such sophistry in my life," said Ralph in disgust. "You'll be telling us next," he added sarcastically, "that we hadn't any right to capture them."

"We hadn't," Frank replied promptly. "On

reflection, I consider that the second greatest crime of my existence. But that's done and can't be wiped out. They own this island just as much as we do. They'd been coming to it for months before we saw it. They ought to have every kind of right and freedom and privilege on it that we have."

" I'd like to hear," Addington said in the high, thin tone of his peevish disgust, " the evidence that justifies you in saying that. What have they ever done on this island to put them on an equality with us? Aren't they our inferiors from every point of view, especially physically? "

" Certainly they are," agreed Honey, not peevishly but as one who indorses, unnecessarily, a self-evident fact. " They've lived here on Angel Island as long as we have. But they haven't made good yet, and we have. Why, just imagine them working on the New Camp—playing tennis, even."

" But we prevented all that," Frank protested. " We cut their wings. Handicapped as they were by their small feet, they could do nothing."

"But," Honey ejaculated, "if they'd been our physical equals, they would never have let us cut their wings."

"But we caught them with a trick," Frank said, "we put them in a position in which they could not use their physical strength."

"Well, if they'd been our mental equals, they'd never let themselves get caught like that."

"Well—but—but—but——" Frank sputtered. "Now you're arguing crazily. You're going round in a circle."

"Oh, well," Honey exclaimed impatiently, "let's not argue any more. You always go round in a circle. I hate argument. It never changes anybody. You never hear what the other fellow says. You always come out of it with your convictions strengthened."

Frank made a gesture of despair. He drew a little book from his pocket and began to read.

"There's one thing about them that certainly is to laugh," Honey said after a silence, a glint of amusement in his big eyes, "and that is the care they take of those useless feet of theirs.

Lulu's even taken to doing hers up every night in oil or cream. It's their particular vanity. Now take that, for instance. Men never have those petty vanities. I mean real men—regular fellows."

" How about the western cowboy and his fancy boots? " Frank shot back over his book.

" Oh, that's different," Ralph said. " Honey's right. That business of taking care of their feet symbolizes the whole sex to me. They do the things they do just because the others do them— like sheep jumping over a wall. Their fad at present is pedicure. Peachy's at it just like the rest of them. Every night when I come home, I find her sitting down with both feet done up in one of those beautiful scarfs she's collected, resting on a cushion. It's rather amusing, though." Ralph struggled to suppress his smile of appreciation.

" Clara's the same." Pete smiled too. " She's cut herself out some high sandals from a pair of my old boots. And she wears them day and night. She says she's been careless lately about getting her feet sunburned. And she's not going to let me see them until they're perfectly white and transparent again. She says that small, beautiful, and useless feet were one of the points of beauty with her people."

"Julia's got the bug, too." Billy's eyes lighted with a gleam of tenderness. "Among the things she found in the trunk was a box of white silk stockings and some moccasins. She's taken to wearing them lately. It always puts a crimp in me to get a glimpse of them—as if she'd suddenly become a normal, civilized woman."

"Now that I think of it," Frank again came out of his book. "Chiquita asked me a little while ago for a pair of shoes. She's wearing them all the time now to protect her feet—from the sun she says."

"It is the most curious thing," Billy said, "that they have never wanted to walk. Not that I want them to now," he added hastily. "That's their greatest charm in my eyes—their helplessness. It has a curious appeal. But it is singular that they never even tried it, if only out of curiosity."

"They have great contempt for walking," Honey observed. "And it has never occurred to them, apparently, that they could enjoy themselves so much more if they could only get about freely. Not that I want them to—any more than you. That utter helplessness is, as you say, appealing."

"Oh, well," Ralph said contemptuously, "what can you expect of them? I tell you it's lack of gray matter. They don't cerebrate. They don't co-ordinate. They don't correlate. They have no initiative, no creative faculty, no mental curiosity or reflexes or reactions. They're nothing but an unrelated bunch of instincts, intuitions, and impulses—human nonsense machines! Why if the positions were reversed and we'd lost our wings, we'd have been trying to walk the first day. We'd have been walking better than they by the end of a month."

"I like it just as it is," Pete said contentedly. "They can't fly and they don't want to walk. We always know where to find them."

"Thank God we don't have to consider

that matter," Billy concluded. " Apparently the walking impulse isn't in them. They might some time, by hook or crook, wheedle us into letting them fly a little. But one thing is certain, they'll never take a step on those useless feet."

" Delicate, adorable, useless little feet of theirs," Pete said softly as if he were reciting from an ode.

" There's something moving along the trail, boys," Frank said quietly. " I keep getting glimpses of it through the bushes—white—blue— red and yellow."

The others stopped, petrified. They scowled, bending an intent gaze through the brilliant noon sunshine.

" Sure I get it! " Billy answered in a low tone. " There's something there."

" I don't." Honey shaded his eyes.

" Nor I." Pete squinted.

" Well, I don't see anything," Ralph said impatiently. " But providing you fellows aren't nuts, what the devil can it be? "

" It's——" Billy began. Then, " My God ! "
he ended.

Something white glimmered at the end of the
trail. It grew larger, bulked definitely, filled the
opening.

" Julia ! " Billy gasped.

" And she's—she's——" Honey could not seem
to go on.

" Walking," Billy concluded for him.

" And Peachy ! " Ralph exclaimed.

" And why—and—and——" It was Pete who
stopped for breath this time.

" And she's walking ! " Ralph concluded for
himself.

" And Clara ! " " And Lulu ! " " And Chiquita ! " they greeted each one of the women as
fast as they appeared. And in between them came
again and again their astonished " And walking ! "

The five women were walking, and walking
with no appearance of effort, swiftly, lightly, joyously. Julia, at the head, moved with the frank,
free, swinging gait of an Amazon. Peachy seemed
to flit along the ground; there was in her progress

something of the dipping, curving grace of her flight. Clara glided; her effect of motionless movement was almost obsidian. Chiquita kept the slow, languid gait, both swaying and pulsating, of a Spanish woman. Lulu trotted with the brisk, pleasing activity of a Morgan pony.

Their skirts had been shortened; they rippled away from slim ankles. The swathing, wing-like draperies had disappeared; their slit sleeves fluttered away from bare shoulders. The women did not pause. They came on steadily, their eyes fixed on the group of men.

The faces in that group had changed in expression. Ralph's became black and lowering. Honey looked surprised but interested; his color did not vary; Billy turned a deep brick-red. Pete went white. Frank Merrill alone studied the phenomenon with the cool, critical eye of scientific observation.

The women paused at a little distance where the path dipped to coil around a little knoll. They abandoned the path to climb this knoll; they climbed it with surprising ease; they almost flew up the sides. They stood there silently grouped about Julia. For an instant the two parties gazed at each other.

Then, " What does this mean, Peachy? " Ralph asked sternly.

Julia answered for Peachy.

" It means—rebellion," she said. " It means that we have decided among ourselves that we will not permit you to cut Angela's wings. It means that rather than have you do that, we will leave you, taking our children with us. If you will promise us that you will not cut Angela's wings nor the wings of any child born to us, we in our turn will promise to return to our homes and take our lives up with you just where we left off."

A confused murmur arose from the men. Ralph leaped to his feet. He made a movement in the direction of the women, involuntary but violent.

The women shrank closer to Julia. They turned white, but they waited. Julia did not stir.

" Go home, you——" Ralph stopped abruptly and choked something back.

" Go at once ! " Billy added sternly.

" I'm ashamed of you, Clara," Pete said.

" Better go back, girls," Honey advised.
He tried to make his tone authoritative.
But in spite of himself, there lingered a little
pleading in it. To make up, he unmasked
the full battery of his coaxing smile, his quiz-
zical frown, his snapping dimples. " We
can't let Angela fly after she's grown up. It
isn't natural. It isn't what a woman should be
doing."

Frank said nothing.

Julia looked at them steadily an instant.
" Come ! " she said briefly to her little band. The
women ran down the knoll and disappeared up the
trail.

" Well, I'll be damned," Ralph remarked.

" Well, when you come to that, *I'll* be damned,"
Honey coincided.

" Who was it said that God did not intend them
to walk ? " Frank asked slyly.

" So that's what all this bandaging of feet

meant," Billy went on, ignoring this thrust. "They were learning to walk all the time."

"You're on," Ralph said in a disgusted tone. "Foxy little devils!"

"Gee, it must have hurt!" Honey exclaimed. "They must have been torn to ribbons at first. Some pluck, believe me!"

"I bet you dollars to doughnuts, Julia's at the bottom of it," remarked Pete.

"No question about that," Frank commented. "Julia *thinks*."

"Considerable bean, too," said Honey. "Well, we've got to put a stop to it to-night."

"Sure!" Ralph agreed. "Read the riot act the instant we get home. By the Lord Harry, if it's necessary I'll tie my wife up!"

"I never could do that," said Pete.

"Nor I," said Frank.

"Nor I," said Honey. "But I don't think we'll have to resort to violent measures. We've only got to appeal to their love; I can twist Lulu right round my finger that way."

"I guess you're right," Ralph smiled. "That always fetches them."

"I don't anticipate any real trouble from this," Billy went on as though arguing with himself. "We've got to take it at the start, though. We can't have Angela flying after she's grown."

"Sure," said Honey, "it'll blow over in a few days. But now that they can walk, let's offer to teach them how to dance and play tennis and bocci and golf. And I'll tell you what—we'll lay out some gardens for them—make them think they're beautifying the place. We might even teach them how to put up shelves and a few little carpentering tricks like that. That'll hold them for a while. Oh, you'll all come round to my tactics sooner or later! Pay them compliments! Give them presents! Jolly them along! And say, it will be fun to have some mixed doubles. Gee, though, they'll be something fierce now they've learned how to walk. They'll be here half the time. They'll have so many ideas how the New Camp ought to be built and a woman is such an obstinate cuss.

Asking questions and arguing and interfering—
they delay things so. We've got to find out something harmless that'll keep them busy."

"Oh, we never can have them here—never in
the world," Ralph agreed. "But we'll fix them
to-night. How about it, old top?" he inquired
jovially of Frank.

Frank did not answer.

In point of fact they did not "fix" the women
that night, owing to the simple reason that they
found the camp deserted—not a sign of woman
or child in sight or hearing.

"Well, there's one thing about it," Ralph said
on their way back to the New Camp the next morning, "you can always beat any woman's game by
just ignoring it. They can stand anything but not
being noticed. Now our play is to do nothing and
say nothing. They're on this island somewhere.
They can't walk off it, and they can't swim off it,
and they can't fly off it. They may stay away for
a day or more or possibly two. By the end of
a week they'll certainly be starved out. And

they'll be longing for our society. We want to keep right at work as if nothing had happened. Let them go and come as they please. But we take no notice—see! We've done that once before and we can do it again. When they come home, they'll be a pretty tired-out, hungry, discouraged gang of girls. I bet we never hear another word out of them on this subject."

The men worked as usual the whole morning; but they talked less. They were visibly preoccupied. At every pause, they glanced furtively up the trail. When noon came, it was evident that they dropped their tools with relief. They sat with their eyes glued to the path.

"Here they come!" Billy exclaimed at last.

The men did not speak; nor until they came to the little knoll that debouched from the trail did the women. Again Julia acted as spokesman. "We have given you a night to think this matter over," she said briefly. "What is your decision? Shall Angela's wings go uncut?"

"No, by God!" burst out Ralph. "No daughter of mine is going to fly. If you——"

But with a silencing gesture, Billy interposed. "Aren't you women happy?" he asked.

"Oh, no," Julia answered. "Of course we're not. I mean we have one kind of happiness—the happiness that comes from being loved and having a home and children. But there is another kind of happiness of which when you cut our wings we were no longer capable—the happiness that comes from a sense of absolute freedom. We can bear that for ourselves, but not for our daughters. Angela and all the girl-children who follow her must have the freedom that we have lost. Will you give it to them?"

"No!" Ralph yelled. And "Go home!" Honey said brutally.

The women turned.

A dead tree grew by the knoll, one slender limb stretching across its top to the lake. Peachy ran nimbly along this limb until she came as near to the tip as her weight would permit. She stood there an instant balancing herself; then she walked swiftly back and forth. Finally she jumped to the ground, landing squarely on her feet. She ran like a deer to join the file of women.

Involuntarily the men applauded.

" Remember the time when they first came to the island," Ralph said, " how she was proud like a lion because she managed to hold herself for an instant on a tree-branch? Her wings were helping her then. Now it's a real balancing act. Some stunt that! By Jove, she must have been practising tight-rope walking." In spite of his scowl, a certain tenderness, half of past admiration, half of present pride, gleamed in his eyes.

" You betchu they have. They've been practising running and jumping and leaping and vaulting and God only knows what else. Well, we've only got to keep this up two or three days longer and they'll come back." Honey spoke in a tone which palpably he tried to make jaunty. In spite of himself, there was a wavering note of uncertainty in it.

" Oh, we'll get them yet!" Ralph said. " How about it, old fellow?" Ralph had never lost his old habit of turning to Frank in psychological distress.

But Frank again kept silence.

" Betchu we find them at home to-night," Honey said as they started down the trail an hour ahead of time. " Who'll take me. Come ! "

No one took him, luckily for Honey. There was no sign of life that night, nor the next, nor the next. And in the meantime, the women did not manifest themselves once during the daytime at the New Camp.

" God, we've got to do something about this," Ralph said at the end of five days. " This is getting serious. I want to see Angela. I hadn't any idea I could miss her so much. It seems as if they'd been gone for a month. They must have been preparing for this siege for weeks. Where the thunder are they hiding—in the jungle somewhere, of course ? "

" Oh, of course," Honey assented. " I miss the boys, too," he mourned, " I used to have a frolic with them every morning before I left and every night when I got home."

"And it's all so uncomfortable living alone," Ralph grumbled. He was unshaven. The others showed in various aspects of untidiness the lack of female standards.

"I'm so sick of my own cooking," Honey complained.

"Not so sick as we are," said Pete.

"Anybody can have my job that wants it," Honey volunteered with a touch of surliness unusual with him.

At noon the five women appeared again at the end of the trail.

In contrast to the tired faces and dishevelled figures of the men, they presented an exquisite feminine freshness, hair beautifully coiled, garments spotless and unwrinkled. But although their eyes were like stars and their cheeks like flowers, their faces were serious; a dew, as of tears lately shed, lay over them.

"Shall Angela fly?" Julia asked without parley.

"No!" Addington yelled.

The women turned.

"Wait a moment," Frank called in a sudden tone of authority. "I'm with you women in this. If you'll let me join your forces, I'll fight on your side."

He had half-covered the distance between them before Julia stopped him with a "Wait a moment!" as decisive as his own.

"In the first place," she said, "we don't want your help. If we don't get this by our own efforts, we'll never value it. In the second place, we'll never be sure of it. We don't trust you—quite. You tricked us once. That was your fault. If you trick us again, that's our fault. Thank you—but no, Frank."

The women disappeared down the trail while still the men stood staring.

"Well, can you beat it?" was the only comment for a moment—and that came from Pete. In another instant, they had turned on Merrill, were upbraiding him hotly for what they called his treason.

"You can't bully me," was his unvarying answer. " Remember, any time they call on me, I'll fight for them."

" Well, you can do what you want with your own wife, of course," Ralph said, falling into one of his black rages. " But I'm damned if you'll encourage mine."

" Boys," he added later, after a day of steadily increasing rage, " I'm tired of this funny business. Let's knock off work to-morrow and hunt them. What gets me is their simplicity. They don't seem to have calculated on our superior strength. It won't take us more than a few hours to run them to earth. By God, I wish we had a pair of bloodhounds."

" All right," said Billy. " I'm with you, Ralph. I'm tired of this."

" Let's go to bed early to-night," said Pete, " and start at sunrise."

" Well," said Honey philosophically, " I've hunted deer, bear, panther, buffalo, Rocky Mountain sheep, jaguar, lion, tiger, and rhinoceros— but this is the first time I ever hunted women."

They started at sunrise—all except Frank, who

refused to have anything to do with the expedition—and they hunted all day. At sunset they camped where they fell exhausted. They went back to the search the next day and the next and the next and the next.

And nowhere did they find traces of their prey.

"Where are they?" Ralph said again and again in a baffled tone. "They couldn't have flown away, could they?"

And, as often as he asked this question, his companions answered it in the varying tones of their fatigue and their despair. "Of course they couldn't—their wings were too short."

"Still," Frank said once. "It's now long past the half-yearly shearing period." He added in another instant, "I don't think, though, that their wings could more than lift them."

"Well, it's evident, wherever they are, they won't budge until we go back to work," Billy said at the end of a week. "This is useless and hopeless."

The next day they returned to the New Camp.

"Here they come," Billy called joyously that noon. "Thank God!" he added under his breath.

Again the five women appeared at the beginning of the trail. Their faces were white now, hollow and lined; but as ever, they bore a look of extraordinary pristineness. And this time they brought the children. Angela lay in her mother's arms like a wilted flower. Her wings sagged forlornly and her feet were bandaged. But stars of a brilliant blue flared and died and flared again in her eyes; roses of a living flame bloomed and faded and bloomed again in her cheek. Her look went straight to her father's face, clung there in luminous entreaty. Peterkin, more than ever like a stray from some unreal, pixy world, surveyed the scene with his big, wondering, gray-green eyes. Honey-Boy, having apparently just waked, stared, owl-like, his brows pursed in comic reproduction of his father's expression. Junior grinned his widest grin and padded the air unceasingly with his pudgy hands. Honey-Bunch slept placidly in Julia's arms.

Julia advanced a little from her group and dropped a single monosyllable. " Well? " she said in an inflexible, questioning voice.

Nobody answered her. Instead Addington called in a beseeching voice: " Angela ! Angela ! Come to me ! Come to dad, baby ! "

Angela's dead little wings suddenly flared with life ; they fluttered in a very panic. She stretched out her arms to her father. She turned her limpid gaze in an agony of infantile entreaty up to her mother's face. But Peachy shook her head. The baby flutter died down. Angela closed her eyes, dropped her head on her mother's shoulder; the tears started from under her eyelids.

" Shall Angela fly? " Julia asked. " Remember this is your last chance."

" No," Ralph said. And the word was the growl of a balked beast.

" Then," Julia said sternly, " we will leave Angel Island forever."

" You will," Ralph sneered. " You will, will you? All right. Let's see you do it ! " Suddenly he started swiftly down toward the trail. " Come, boys!" he commanded. Honey followed—and Billy and Pete.

But, suddenly, Julia spoke. She spoke in the loud, clear tones of her flying days and she used the language of her girlhood. It was a word of command. And as it fell from her lips, the five women leaped from the top of the knoll. But they did not fall into the lake. They did not touch its surface. They flew. Flew—and yet it was not flight. It was half-flight. It was scarcely flight at all. Compared with the magnificent, calm, effortless sweep of their girlhood days, it was almost a grotesque performance. Their wing-stumps beat back and forth violently, beat in a very agony of effort. Indeed these stunted fans could never have held them up. They supplemented their efforts by a curious rotary movement of the legs and feet. They could not rise very far above the surface of the water, especially as each woman was weighted by a child; but they sustained a steady, level flight to the other side of the lake.

The men stared for an instant, petrified. Then

panic broke. " Come back, Lulu ! " Honey yelled.
" Come back ! " " Julia ! " Billy called hoarsely,
" Julia ! Julia ! Julia ! " He went on calling her
name as if his senses had left him. Pete's lips
moved. Words came, but no voice; he stood like
a statue, whispering. Merrill remained silent;
obviously he could not even whisper; his was the
silence of paralysis. Addington, on the other hand,
was all voice. " Oh, my God ! " he cried. " Don't
leave me, Peachy ! Don't leave me ! Peachy !
Angela ! Peachy ! Angela ! " His voice ascended
on the scale of hysteric entreaty until he screeched.
" Don't leave me ! Don't leave me ! " He fell to
his knees and held out his arms; the tears poured
down his face.

The women heard, turned, flew back. Holding themselves above the men's heads, they fluttered and floated. Their faces were working
and the tears flowed freely, but they kept
their eyes steadily fixed on Julia, waiting for
command.

Julia was ghastly. " Shall Angela fly ? " she
asked. And it was as though her voice came from

an enormous distance, so thin and expressionless
and far-away had it become.

"Anything!" Addington said. "Anything!
Oh, my God, don't leave us!"

Julia said something. Again this word was in
their own language and again it was a word of
command. But emotion had come into her voice
—joy; it thrilled through the air like a magic
fluid. The women sank slowly to earth. In another instant the two forces were in each other's
arms.

"Billy," Julia said, as hand in hand they struck
into one of the paths that led to the jungle, "will
you marry me?"

Billy did not answer. He only looked at her.

"When?" he said finally. "To-morrow?"

"To-day," Julia said.

Sunset on Angel Island.

The Honeymoon House thrilled with excitement. At intervals figures crowded to the narrow
door; at intervals faces crowded in the narrow

window. Sometimes it was Lulu, swollen and purple and broken with weeping. Sometimes it was Chiquita, pale and blurred and sagging with tears. Often it was Peachy, whose look, white and sodden, steadily searched the distance. Below on the sand, Clara, shriveled, pinched, bent over, her hands writhing in and out of each other's clasp, paced back and forth, her eye moving always on the path. Suddenly she stopped and listened. There came first a faint disturbance of the air, then confusion, then the pounding of feet. Angela, white-faced, frightened, appeared, flying above the trail. " I found him," she called. Behind came Billy, running. He flashed past Clara. " How is she? " he panted.

" Alive," Clara said briefly.

He flew up the steps. Clara followed. Angela dropped to the sand and lay there, her little head in the crook of her elbow, sobbing.

Inside a murmur of relief greeted Billy. " He's come, Julia," Peachy whispered softly.

The women withdrew from the inner room as Billy passed over the threshold.

Julia lay on the couch stately and still. One long white hand rested on her breast. The other stretched at her side; its fingers touched a little bundle there. Her wings—the glorious pinions of her girlhood—towered above the pillow, silver-shining, quiescent. Her honey-colored hair piled in a huge crown above her brow. Her eyes were closed. Her face was like marble; but for an occasional faint movement of the hand at her side, she might have been the sculpture on a tomb.

Her lids flickered as Billy approached, opened on eyes as dull as stones. But as they looked up into his, they filled with light.

"My husband——" she said. Her eyes closed.

But presently they opened and with a greater dazzle of light. "Our son——" The hand at her side moved feebly on the little bundle there. That faint movement seemed a great effort. Her eyes closed again.

But for a third time she opened them, and now they shone with their greatest glory. "My husband—our son—has—wings."

And then Julia's eyes closed for the last time.

LOST RACE AND ADULT FANTASY FICTION

An Arno Press Collection

Ames, Joseph Bushnell. **The Bladed Barrier.** 1929

Anderson, Olof W. **The Treasure Vault of Atlantis.** 1925

Arnold, Edwin Lester. **Lepidus the Centurion.** 1901

[Atkins, Frank]. Frank Aubrey, pseud. **The Devil-Tree of El Dorado.** 1897

[Atkins, Frank]. Frank Aubrey, pseud. **King of the Dead:**
A Weird Romance. 1903

Bennet, Robert Ames. **Thyra:** A Romance of the Polar Pit. 1901

[Bennett, Gertrude Barrows]. Francis Stevens, pseud.
The Heads of Cerberus. 1952

Blackwood, Algernon. **The Fruit Stoners.** 1935

[Boëx, Joseph-Henri]. J.-H. Rosny aîne, pseud. **The Xipehuz** *and*
The Death of the Earth. Translated from the original 1888 and 1912
French editions by George Edgar Slusser. 1978

Bruce, Muriel. **Mukara.** 1930

[Burton, Alice Elizabeth]. Susan Alice Kerby, pseud.
Miss Carter and the Ifrit. [1945]

Carew, Henry. **The Vampires of the Andes.** 1925

Chambers, Robert. **The Slayer of Souls.** 1920

Channing, Mark. **White Python:** Adventure and Mystery in Tibet. 1934

Chester, George Randolph. **The Jingo.** 1912

Clock, Herbert and Eric Boetzel. **The Light in the Sky.** 1929

Coblentz, Stanton A[rthur]. **When the Birds Fly South.** 1945

Constantine, Murray, pseud. **The Devil, Poor Devil!** 1934

Cook, William Wallace. **Cast Away at the Pole.** 1904

Cowan, Frank. **Revi-Lona:** A Romance of Love in a
Marvelous Land. [c. 1890]

Day, Bradford M., compiler and editor. **Bibliography of Adventure:**
Mundy, Burroughs, Rohmer, Haggard. Revised edition. 1978

de Comeau, Alexander. **Monk's Magic.** 1931

[de Grainville, Jean Baptiste François Xavier Cousin]. **The Last Man, Or,**
Omegarus and Syderia. Two vols. in one. 1806/1806

Dunn, J. Allan. **The Flower of Fate.** 1928

Eddison, E[ric] R[ucker]. **Styrbiorn the Strong.** 1926

Fleckenstein, Alfred C. **The Prince of Gravas.** 1898

Fyne, Neal, pseud. **The Land of the Living Dead.** [1897]

Gillmore, Inez Haynes. **Angel Island.** 1914

[Gompertz, Martin Louis Alan]. "Ganpat," pseud. **Adventures in**
Sakaeland Comprising Harilek *and* **Wrexham's Romance.**
Two vols. in one. 1923/1935

Green, Fitzhugh. **Z R Wins.** 1924

[Gregory, Jackson]. Quien Sabe, pseud. **Daughter of the Sun.** 1921

Griffith [-Jones], George [Chetwynd]. **The Romance of**
Golden Star.... 1897

[Guthrie, Thomas Anstey]. F. Anstey, pseud. **Humour & Fantasy.** 1931

Haggard, H[enry] Rider. **The Mahatma and the Hare.** 1911

Haggard, H[enry] Rider. **Wisdom's Daughter.** 1923

Haldane, Charlotte. **Melusine or Devil Take Her!** [1936]

[Harris-Burland, John Burland]. Harris Burland, pseud.
The Princess Thora. 1904

Hartmann, Franz. **Among the Gnomes.** 1895

Hodder, William Reginald. **Daughter of the Dawn.** 1903

Knowles, Vernon. **Sapphires: Here and Otherwhere** *and* **Silver Nutmegs.** Two vols. in one. 1926/1927

Kummer, Frederic Arnold. **Shades of Hades: Ladies in Hades** *and* **Gentlemen in Hades.** Two vols. in one. 1930/1930

Large, E. C. **Asleep in the Afternoon.** 1939

Le Queux, William [Tufnell]. **The Eye of Istar.** 1897

Leroux, Gaston. **The Bride of the Sun.** 1915

Lindsay, David. **Devil's Tor.** 1932

Linklater, Eric. **A Spell For Old Bones.** 1950

London, Jack. **Hearts of Three.** 1920

[Lunn, Hugh Kingsmill]. Hugh Kingsmill, pseud. **The Return of William Shakespeare.** 1929

Marshall, Sidney J. **The King of Kor;** Or, She's Promise Kept. 1903

McHugh, Vincent. **I Am Thinking of My Darling.** 1943

Menville, Douglas and R. Reginald, editors. **Dreamers of Dreams:** An Anthology of Fantasy. 1978

Menville, Douglas and R. Reginald, editors. **Worlds of Never:** Three Fantastic Novels. 1978

Merritt, A[braham]. **The Fox Woman and Other Stories.** 1949

Morris, Kenneth. **Book of the Three Dragons.** 1930

Murray, G. G. A. **Gobi or Shamo.** 1889

Owen, Frank. **The Purple Sea.** 1930

Potter, Margaret Horton. **Istar of Babylon.** 1902

Reginald, R. and Douglas Menville, editors. **King Solomon's Children:** Some Parodies of H. Rider Haggard. 1978

Reginald, R. and Douglas Menville, editors. **They: Three Parodies of** H. Rider Haggard's *She.* With an Introduction by R. Reginald. 1978

Rolfe, Frederick [William] and [Charles Harry Clinton Pirie-Gordon].
Prospero and Caliban, pseuds. **Hubert's Arthur.** 1935

Savile, Frank. **Beyond the Great South Wall.** 1901

Scott, G. Firth. **The Last Lemurian.** 1898

Sheldon-Williams, Miles. **The Power of Ula.** 1906

Sinclair, Upton. **Prince Hagen.** 1903

[Smith, Ernest Bramah]. Ernest Bramah, pseud. **Kai Lung Beneath the Mulberry-Tree.** 1940

Todd, Ruthven. **Over the Mountain.** 1939

Vivian, E[velyn] Charles. **Aia: Fields of Sleep** *and*
People of the Darkness. Two vols. in one. [1925]/1924

Vivian, E[velyn] Charles. **A King There Was--.** [1926]

Wells, H[erbert] G[eorge]. **The Wonderful Visit.** 1895